DESOLATION CANYON

RUSSELL JAMES

SEVEREDPRESS

DESOLATION CANYON

Copyright © 2023 Russell James

WWW.SEVEREDPRESS.COM

ISBN: 978-1-922861-96-2

Other books by Russell James

Grant Coleman Adventures

Cavern of the Damned

Monsters in the Clouds

Curse of the Viper King

Forest of Fire

Mammoth Island

Atoll X

Ranger Kathy West National Park Adventures

Claws

Dragons of Kilauea

Ravens of Yellowstone

Rick and Rose Sinclair Adventures

Quest for the Queen's Temple

Voyage to Blackbeard's Island

DEDICATION

For Christy,
You are right about not wanting to live in a cliffside house.

CHAPTER ONE

July 3, 2019

Renata Suárez knew she'd just found the ultimate thrill.

She stood on the edge of a narrow canyon that wasn't on any of the maps. It stretched out several miles north and south of where she stood; the curves in it made it hard to tell how far. It only seemed a few hundred yards wide here, but overhangs on both sides made that distance look deceptively small. The canyon was much wider at the bottom, several hundred feet down. A river rushed down the canyon's center. Around it grew an amazingly dense collection of trees and bushes, especially considering that the area around the canyon rim was a sandy wasteland.

She'd been on her way across this section of the Utah desert in search of adventure. She'd heard about a butte west of here that few had visited. Her plan had been to free climb to the top, followed by a base jump back down to her truck. She hadn't had a cell signal during the last hour of driving, so live streaming the event to her fans at GoDaredevilGirl.com was out. Instead she'd video the hell out of it and post the footage as soon as she got back to civilization.

But then she found this canyon. Had she been less attentive, she'd have driven into it. This was a much better location for the stunt. It was beautiful, it was mysterious, and she was the only one who knew about it. All she needed to do differently was to reverse her plan. Do the base jump down to the bottom first, then the free climb back up.

Her skin tingled over how awesome this reel was going to be. She'd double her followers and land some high-paying sponsors for sure after it all went viral.

Renata stood at the rim suited up and ready. The overhang made the whole endeavor much easier. Some supplies and her free-climb tools filled the backpack at her feet. The last thing she needed on a base jump like this was a ton of extra weight. She'd tied the tiny drogue chute from her parachute to the top to slow its fall, but nothing inside was fragile.

She tossed the pack over the cliff. The chute popped open, but the pack still plummeted straight down. It landed with a loud crash on a bush at the bottom.

Some branches seemed to sway by the river in response to the noise. But it was hard for her to tell at this height, and she'd seen the wind do the same thing to trees a hundred times. She was too psyched up about the jump to worry about it.

Now it was her turn.

She flicked on the camera attached to her helmet.

"Okay, Daredevilistas! Sit back and enjoy one awesome drop into a secret canyon."

She sprinted for the edge and launched herself into the air. With no concern about bouncing off the cliff wall, she indulged herself by executing a forward somersault before falling chest-first. She knew the helmet-view video of the world turning upside down would get tons of likes.

Renata spread her arms and legs and pulled her chute. It zipped out above her and then expanded like a blooming flower. She rotated feet-first and started looking for a landing spot.

She cursed loud enough that she was sure her camera picked it up. Problem Number One was that without the drogue chute, her parachute had opened slower, and she was much lower than expected. Problem Number Two was that she was nowhere near a clearing. Landing in a tree risked broken bones and the chance of being stuck in it until she starved to death.

A river landing was an option.

And an awful option it was. Slick rocks meant no good footing. The water might be so deep she couldn't touch bottom. The current might be so swift she'd be unable to stand up. The parachute might drag her downriver or land atop her and drown her.

But it still beat a tree landing.

Renata yanked hard on the risers and angled herself for the water.

A few yards ahead, one tree stood dead center in her path. She was going to glide right into it. As she closed on it, a startled bird exploded from the topmost branches and flew off. Renata was so close she could make out every feather.

She tucked her knees up until they nearly touched her chin. It wasn't enough. She hit the top of the tree and snapped off the peak. The jagged tip of the trunk ripped her pants and slashed her butt. It felt like someone had carved her with a hot knife.

Renata had cleared the tree, but the impact had made her fall faster. She gave the risers a few steering tugs and aimed for a landing facing north against the current. The river bubbled with the kind of frothy ripples that promised nasty boulders beneath the surface. She aimed for the calmest spot.

Renata dropped her feet as she hit the water. It was surprisingly cold, and surprisingly fast. The soles of her shoes hit the rocky river bottom. The water was only armpit deep. She sighed with relief.

Then the parachute hit the water behind her. The current re-inflated it. It took off like a greyhound out of a starting gate, yanked her off her feet, and sent her back-first into the river.

She went under and water rushed into her mouth. Her hands flailed for the chute release, found it, and pressed. The chute swam downstream without her. Her head broke the surface and she got her feet on the river bottom again. Renata coughed up a big slug of water and spat it out.

The panic of the moment drained away. She smiled as the ecstasy of survival took its place. She'd damn-near died, but that was the whole point. There wasn't any rush without a ton of risk. She popped her helmet off her head and flipped it around so the camera faced her.

"Whoa, Daredevilistas! That was some hairy ride. It might have looked scary, but I had it totally under control at all times. Still, don't try that at home. Let's play it back in slow motion and I'll walk you through it."

She shut off the camera. It was going to be fun editing this all together.

Upstream, something splashed.

She lowered her helmet and looked in that direction. All she saw was rushing river. Renata rationalized that that was what made the noise she'd heard.

3

Then something long and dark surfaced just upstream. At first glance she thought it was a log about five feet long with bumpy bark. But while the water moved, it did not. Could it have snagged on something? Could the water be so much shallower so close to her?

Two of the upstream bumps opened up and revealed a pair of eyes with red, slit pupils.

Renata's blood ran cold. The thing didn't look like a log at all now. She knew a crocodile when she saw one, even if it was three times too large. The creature moved in her direction.

She turned to run for shore. But the current was strong and she was up to her armpits in water. Her limbs moved in slow motion while her heart pounded at triple speed.

A deep bellow rolled across the river. Renata seemed to move even slower against the current.

She risked a quick look over her shoulder.

A set of crocodile jaws opened wide. Rows of white, pointed teeth glistened in the sun. An awful stench came from within the creature, one that Renata could only associate with death.

The giant crocodile struck and clamped onto Renata's arm. It dragged her under. She dropped her helmet. The current caught it and it bounced southward along the riverbed.

The crocodile executed an underwater spin like a chicken on a rotisserie. Renata's arm ripped away and her shoulder joint shattered. She screamed in pain, but the river muffled her cry, and then forced itself down her throat and into her lungs.

Her last big thrill ended.

***

At the south end of the canyon, her helmet bounced into the cavern where the river disappeared. The camera struck a rock and shattered. It would forever keep Renata's fate a secret.

CHAPTER TWO

Present Day

Professor Grant Coleman smiled, happy in his element.

He stood at the front of the lecture hall. The sixty-six nervous students of his Introduction to Paleontology class filled the seats. He'd only lost four over the semester, and all of them were gone because they had left Robeson College for family emergencies, not because they were failing his class. He was proud that he always failed so few. He made it a point to make the lectures interesting enough to attend, and he and his teaching assistants available if anyone needed some help.

Grant left administering the exam in the hands of his graduate students and returned to his office. Inside, piles of files and reference books teetered on every flat surface. If anyone asked, Grant would blame the room's cluttered catastrophe on the end-of-semester rush. In reality, it always looked this way, and sometimes it looked worse. He hadn't been able to use the last break between semesters to get organized. Instead, he'd spent it trying to not be eaten by prehistoric monsters on a Pacific atoll.

The sad part was, that hadn't been the first time he'd gotten into that kind of a scrape. His paleontological expertise had opened a number of doors throughout his career and lately he'd been finding giant monsters behind many of them. With any luck, his Atoll X misadventure would be his last. He much preferred his giant creatures in a fossilized form. They had never tried to kill him.

Grant rearranged a few piles to make space on his desk. He took a seat and cleaned his glasses. Then he opened the folder containing the tests from his graduate paleontology class, and began to read the essays.

The desk phone rang. The caller ID revealed the caller was his literary agent, Harvey Rindzunner. The upside to Grant's near-death adventures was that he'd turned fictionalized versions of them into novels. Harvey had been able to get his previous manuscripts published. Grant couldn't quit his day job, and didn't want to, but the extra income kept his ex-wife's alimony payments up to date.

Grant picked up the phone. "Harvey! What a surprise."

"I told you I'd call today," Harvey said.

"That's what makes it such a surprise. You usually lie about that."

"Grant, you wound me with your words. Deeply. Especially when I'm bringing you such good news. I sold *Atoll X* to the publisher and got you a sweet advance."

That *was* good news. That manuscript was the thinly-veiled autobiographical story of the Pacific atoll adventure he'd recently survived. Despite the fact that most of the events were true, he was afraid they would be too unbelievable to get published, even in a novel.

"The editors asked me," Harvey said, "these giant monsters you keep coming up with, where do you get the inspiration?"

"You know, I'm just minding my own business, leading a normal life, and then suddenly they appear right in front of me."

"Well, do whatever you need to do to keep those inspirational moments coming."

Grant would really prefer that he didn't. A monster-free future would suit him just fine.

"I got a line on a consulting gig for your semester break," Harvey said. "There's a guy in—"

"Stop right there," Grant cut him off. "The mess in the Pacific on Nirvana Island ended your vacation planner status for me. You focus on scaring up publishing and media deals. If I want to travel somewhere, I'll use an online booking agency."

"This is easy money."

"That's what you said about Nirvana Island. Hard pass."

"You're killing me, Grant." A phone rang in the background. "Gotta get that call. Talk later."

Harvey hung up.

Grant's boss, Dean Malley, entered Grant's office. The stooped, older man had a long nose that Grant thought spent too much time being poked into his curriculum and teaching methods.

He wore a dark suit sporting a plastic breast pocket name badge adorned with the college logo. The dean only wore that badge when he was greeting alumni, which reminded Grant that there had been an alumni luncheon that day, which reminded Grant he was supposed to have attended it.

"Dean Malley! Your unannounced visits are always a treat."

"You missed the alumni luncheon. I'm disappointed in you."

"As am I. It's not like me to forget about free food."

"Making alumni contacts will go a long way in helping keep your employer well-funded, you know."

"I've seen the size of Robeson University's endowment," Grant said. "Contrary to what the size of my paycheck would indicate, the university isn't broke."

"One of the alumni announced he was sponsoring a geological study in the Southwest," Dean Malley said. "He appointed Casey Palmer to lead it."

Professor Casey Palmer and Grant were friends. Casey was the university's top geology professor and frequently did consulting work. Casey and Grant had a lot of overlapping professional interests. They swapped guest lecture slots in each other's classes at least once a semester. Casey had grown up in a coal mining family in West Virginia and had worked his way through six years of college by going home to the mines every summer to earn his tuition.

"Maybe if you networked with the alumni more," Dean Malley said, "someone might steer an opportunity like that your way."

Grant wanted to reply that the last "opportunity" he'd just experienced had damn near killed him on several occasions. "I'll keep that in mind."

"Another high-profile expedition tied to the university would sure make me proud."

"Making you proud is my whole reason for living," Grant said.

Dean Malley rolled his eyes and departed. A few minutes later, Casey Palmer entered Grant's office. He was Grant's age but taller. He still carried a trace of a southern accent and the lean look of someone who'd made a living doing hard work. His hair had much more than a touch of gray to it. He was beaming.

"You weren't at the luncheon," he said.

"You're the second person to be concerned about me missing a meal. Do I look emaciated?"

Casey eyed Grant's paunchy belly. "Hardly. But I did get some good news there."

"That you'll be leading an all-expenses paid trip to study rocks in the desert?"

Casey's eyes widened. "How did you know? It was just announced."

"Crystal ball. Tea leaves. Chicken bones. I have my ways."

"You don't know the best part of the deal. You get to come along as well, all expenses paid."

"And why would I want to go look at rocks in the desert?" Grant said.

"Along with the geology they told me about, the company mentioned that earthquakes exposed some interesting fossils in the same remote desert canyon. I immediately thought of you."

Grant's ears perked up and he set down his pen. Having had enough of oceans, lagoons, and murderous aquatic life to last a lifetime, the desert sounded wonderful. And he'd just been thinking how much he missed the thrill of fossil discovery. "That offer sounds interesting. The company would pay for me to join this trip?"

"The company put me in charge of the dig, so in my infinite authority, I grant you permission to join it."

Grant placed a hand on his chest and leaned forward. "I bow down before the ruler of the dig."

"The expedition is going to a spot called Desolation Canyon, in an area northeast of the Grand Canyon complex. The sponsor doesn't care about fossils, so I'll let you take any you find back to the university."

Now Grant was very interested. Some new fossils would keep him and his grad students engaged and excited for over a semester.

"Look," Casey said, "I'll email you all the details and make all the travel arrangements. It will be great!"

Casey departed. Grant turned to his computer and called up a map of Utah. He couldn't find anywhere named Desolation Canyon. In fact, a lot of the area northeast of the Grand Canyon was just a big empty space on the map, without even any real terrain details to it. Whatever was there, no one had likely seen it before.

After his Nirvana Island nightmare, this trip would be the perfect tonic. Dry, quiet, and above all, monster-free. What could go wrong?

He realized that was the same thought he had before he left to go to Nirvana Island.

CHAPTER THREE

The next day, Grant headed to the teacher's cafeteria for lunch. As he entered the line to order, Casey Parker stepped over and joined him.

"Grant! I was going to come by your office later to see you, but looks like I got lucky."

"And having used all your luck so foolishly, the lotto ticket you bought this morning is now officially a loser."

They grabbed trays and made their way down the line. At the sandwich station, Casey ordered a turkey sub. Grant countered with a double cheeseburger and onion rings.

"Whoa," Casey said. "You only order that when you are in too good a mood to sweat your cholesterol numbers."

"You have that right," Grant said. "And I'll be adding at least one piece of apple pie to this feast as well."

"Did your ex re-marry and end your alimony payments?"

"No, that would call for a triple cheeseburger with bacon. I'm just excited about the potential finds in our upcoming dig. The area you mentioned is prime real estate for Triassic era fossils."

As they made their way to the cashier at the end of the line, Casey filled Grant in on the travel details. Flights were booked for both of them into Salt Lake City, and from there they'd get transported to the site. After paying for lunch, they scanned the crowded cafeteria for somewhere to sit.

"Over there," Casey said.

The table he pointed to had one occupant, Priya Maharaj. The slim Indian woman taught classes on indigenous peoples around the globe. She was eating a salad as she scrolled through something on her tablet, doing both with the elegance of a Hollywood star. Grant thought she did everything like a Hollywood star, though he didn't share that belief with anyone, especially Priya.

"No," Grant said. "I don't want to interrupt Priya."

"Does she really intimidate you that much?"

"Intimidate? Me? Why I laugh at her aristocratic good looks and Rhode-scholar intellect."

"You've let your trainwreck of a divorce make you gun-shy. C'mon. It's about time you made an impression."

"I'm certain I already have. An underwhelming impression, but I'm sure it was made."

Casey led him over to the table. "Mind if we join you?"

"Go right ahead," she said.

Grant set down his tray beside hers. A spoonful of hummus sat atop her crisp salad seasoned with vinegar and herbs. On Grant's plate, the top cheeseburger patty had slid off the bottom one and exposed a greasy puddle atop the meat. He could feel the fat from his meal oozing from his pores and he hadn't even touched it yet. Grant took a seat.

Priya looked at Grant with the unimpressed look he had completely expected. She moved her salad to the far end of her tray, as if the aroma of Grant's fat-festival food choice would wilt her salad leaves. Grant just managed a sheepish, apologetic grin.

"Priya," Casey said, "you got all the details for the trip?"

Grant took a huge bite of cheeseburger. His tastebuds genuflected down in thanks.

She smiled at Casey. "Yes, my flight to Salt Lake will work out perfectly."

"Salt Lake?" Grant said around a mouthful of Grade A beef.

"We're all flying into the same airport," Casey said. "Priya will be on the dig as well."

Grant nearly spat his cheeseburger all over the table. "Priya? Really?"

"The undiscovered canyon may have more than dinosaur fossils in it," Casey said. "It may have artifacts from early Native Americans."

"These were supposedly Anasazi lands," Priya said.

Grant gave her a blank stare as he teetered between pretending he knew what she was talking about and just admitting his ignorance.

Priya seemed to assume the latter. "I devote two lectures to that tribe in my Native American class. They disappeared long before the Spanish arrived."

"I hope you don't blame my dinosaurs." The joke fell flat and Grant wondered if there was room to crawl under the table.

"This dig is in a canyon with walls freshly exposed by an earthquake," Casey said. "That's a geologist's dream come true. Those newly exposed sedimentary layers will tell a hell of a story. I bet I'll write two papers on what we find before you finish picking dinosaur bones out of the dirt."

"Fossils, please," Grant said, "not bones."

"Even if I don't make any finds," Priya said, "I could bring back pictures of the area to add to my Anasazi lectures. You promise to get me back to civilization after a week?"

"Absolutely," Casey said.

"Well, then," Priya said. "Looks like the three of us are going to visit the Southwest."

CHAPTER FOUR

Two weeks later

At first, Grant had entertained some second thoughts about this dig. In his experiences, too good to be true always ended up being just that. So, he'd checked up on the corporation sponsoring the trip, Neoborax Minerals. The publicly-traded company had a market capitalization with almost as many zeros to it as the carbon dates of Grant's fossils. Their website listed holdings that spanned the globe. Being backed by that large a company had put Grant at ease.

After the taxi to the airport arrived on time and his promised extra-legroom seat on the airplane came true, he felt silly for being paranoid about the expedition going sideways. He chalked up his anxiety to the aftertaste of his recent misadventures.

As Grant stood at the baggage claim carousel at Salt Lake City International, the other passengers from his flight crowded around him. Casey and Priya had different flights so he'd been solo on his. Outside, the setting sun reminded him how long his day had been. Between an early start and flight delays and time zone changes, he felt like he'd been traveling forever. The general mood of the rest of the passengers seemed to be the same and they all stared with exasperated anticipation at the idle carousel. If the rest of Grant's travel arrangements were correct, someone named Terri from Neoborax would be waiting for him outside the terminal.

A light flashed and a warning bell sounded. The carousel slithered to life like a great silver serpent, emerging from a set of black strip curtains in the wall, making an upside-down letter omega shape, and then disappearing back into the wall. A moment later, bags began to slide down a chute just this side of the strip curtains.

Grant's lifetime observation was that if it wasn't for bad luck, he'd have no luck at all, so he'd already resigned himself to the fact that his bag would be the last one unloaded from the plane, if it got unloaded at all. He was pleasantly surprised when it popped out through the curtain in the middle of a group of a dozen pink hard-sided suitcases. His roller board bag was small enough to be a carry-on, but he'd opted to let the airline do the work of carting it around the country.

Grant stepped closer to the carousel, ready to lean in and snatch his bag as it passed.

With his bag just six feet away, what seemed like a swarm of short people swept in and surrounded him. They all wore matching baseball hats with the logo of a Chinese tourism firm on the front. They'd filled the entire rear of the plane on the flight out. The air came to life with chattering Mandarin and the surge of the crowd pushed Grant away from the carousel. The group grabbed the pink bags all around Grant's, and then proceeded to do some kind of Boxing Day-type exchange as they traded someone else's suitcase for their own. Grant watched helplessly as his bag passed by well out of reach. By the time the tourist group dispersed, his roller board was on the carousel's other side.

He sighed. At least he knew his bag would come around on a second pass. And with much of the flight having picked up their bags, he'd surely be able to grab it the second time around.

The strips at the far end of the carousel swallowed his suitcase. Moments later, his suitcase reemerged from the mysterious bag handling land on the other side of the wall.

Just as it passed under the delivery slide, a metal suitcase the size of a footlocker came careening down the chute. It T-boned Grant's suitcase and then flopped over to one side. Grant winced. The mangled bag made it to him and he pulled it from the carousel. The frame now had a curve in it the designers never intended. Grant extended the handle with a set of sharp jerks. It too was bent, and the whole thing looked more like an archery bow than a roller board. He set it down and began to pull it toward the exit door. One of the wheels had been crushed, and the suitcase wobbled back and forth so wildly Grant was afraid he'd knock someone over with it.

Outside, a big white SUV with a Neoborax logo on the door idled at the curb. The passenger door opened and out stepped a woman in khakis and a red golf shirt embroidered with the same Neoborax logo. Her dark hair was cut almost as short as Grant's. She was about Grant's height, but looked like she had only half his body mass index.

This woman did not match the mental image he'd painted of Terri. He had to admit to himself he was a little intimidated. He also had to admit that that did not take much.

"Dr. Coleman." She smiled and extended her hand. "I'm Terri Nagle, the liaison for Neoborax."

"Please call me Grant." They shook hands.

"Okay, Grant." She looked at his bag and arched an eyebrow.

"It's a custom bag," Grant said. "Designed by a Robeson College art student. It represents the need to be flexible when traveling."

Terri looked like she was pondering whether to take him seriously. Then she opened the rear door to the SUV and revealed Priya sitting in the third row and Casey sitting in the second.

"Dear Professor, we were starting to worry," Casey said.

"No need to worry. I wasn't doing the flying. It was just the usual delays, plus a few laps of holding so I could savor the recirculated cabin air for a few more precious minutes."

Grant took a seat beside Casey and closed the door. Terri got into the passenger seat. A man also wearing a red Neoborax shift sat in the driver's seat. The instant the doors closed, he pulled out and into traffic.

Terri turned to face Casey. "First things first. You filed the paperwork for the digging permits?"

"Of course," Casey said. "All approved. I've worked with the regulators here before, so they know me."

Grant looked out the window and saw that they were heading out of the city. "What hotel are we staying at tonight?"

"No hotel tonight," Terri said. "We'd lose a whole day that way. Renaldo will drive all night and deliver us to the site by morning."

Grant didn't think that sounded like a relaxing way to get this vacation started. "I was more leaning to spending the evening with a steak dinner followed by a hot shower."

"The team and all the equipment are onsite and ready to start. I'm sure you don't want to waste their day."

"I wasn't thinking of myself as much as my two colleagues here," Grant said. "They're exhausted, I'm sure."

"No, I'm good," Casey said.

Priya wadded up a jacket into a makeshift pillow and wedged it between her seat and the window. "I have slept in far worse situations than this. I will be fine."

Way to back me up, you two, Grant thought. Casey had grown up in the wilds of West Virginia, but he hadn't expected Priya to take roughing it in her stride like this.

"Relax and take a nap," Terri said. "We'll be there by morning."

Everyone leaned back and closed their eyes. Grant's stomach rumbled. He'd seriously planned for a steak dinner tonight, and uncharacteristically eaten just a few snacks during the day so he'd be able to consume the largest one available and savor it. He unzipped the outer pocket of the battered suitcase between his legs and pulled out a shriveled bag of airline peanuts.

His ex-wife used to upbraid him for always squirreling away snacks whenever they went somewhere. This situation was a perfect example of why he did that. He'd throw it back in her face when he returned, except that she'd demanded all contact be through her lawyer. He doubted the lawyer's translation would include his gusto.

He tore open the bag and began to eat the peanuts one by one to stretch out the experience and yes, savor it. When he finished, he leaned back, closed his eyes, and let the thrum of tires on the highway lull him to sleep.

CHAPTER FIVE

Grant suffered a violent awakening.

A sudden lurch by the SUV sent him flying forward and instantly into consciousness. Only his seatbelt kept him from banging into the passenger seat. He steadied himself and then forced his sleep-bleary eyes to focus out the window.

The red hues of sunrise lit the eastern horizon. The SUV's headlights illuminated a pair of ruts on what could only most generously be called a dirt road. The sky was alive with stars, undimmed by the lights of civilization.

Grant looked over at his two compadres, who were still managing to sleep like the dead. He envied them.

Terri glanced back from the passenger seat. She looked annoyingly awake and rested. Grant felt like he'd been sleeping in an iron maiden.

The rising, yellow sun revealed a harsh, desert landscape. Clumps of scattered sagebrush dotted a flat, sandy plain painted in several shades of red. Haze obscured low mountains in the distance.

"If we could stop at the first Waffle House you see for an omelet and a cup of coffee," Grant said, "that would be great."

"There will be food at the camp," Terri said.

Grant's stomach churned at the hope of future sustenance. He decided to try and keep his mind off that. "Tell me about the fossils you've uncovered so far."

"Honestly, I have no idea. A series of earthquakes in the area caused some avalanches along Desolation Canyon. Neoborax is interested in the geology, to look within the sedimentary layer, find proof of past global warming events and their effects."

Grant thought that was awfully progressive thinking for an international mining company. "That's one of Casey's areas of expertise, so you have the right man there to run the show."

"I haven't seen any fossils myself, but they were described as giant lizards with huge heads."

Grant perked up. "A large head generally means a predator. Tyrannosaurs, allosaurs, depending on the age of the stratum. These would be great finds. And if the skeletons are fully articulated, even better. Taking one of those back to the university would make this trip worth every hunger pang it seems bent on inducing."

Up ahead, a set of dun-colored canvas tents appeared.

"Everyone up," she announced. "We're here."

The SUV pulled up to the encampment. As the vehicle came to a stop, Priya and Casey awakened with yawns and stretches.

"You two have perfect timing," Grant said.

"I used to nap on the carts taking us into the mines in West Virginia," Casey said. "I can sleep almost anywhere."

"Good for you," Grant said.

"I'm sure you'll all want to get right to work," Terri said as she opened the door. "The sleeping tent is on the right. You can change, and we'll get you into the canyon."

"After breakfast?" Grant said.

"Yes, after breakfast."

The four of them entered a sleeping tent. As field accommodations went, this one wasn't bad. The cots were cushioned, there were actual pillows, and a solar array provided electricity. Terri explained that the female tent was next door.

"I can get spoiled with this setup," Grant said to Priya and Casey. "Compared to some digs I've been on, this is a five-star hotel."

Priya gave him the same look people give old folks who talk about having to walk to elementary school uphill through the snow.

It looked like most of the rest of the cots were occupied, though none of the occupants were around. "Where's everyone else?" Casey said.

"The team rose before dawn," Terri said, "to be certain all the gear was in the canyon and ready to go when you arrived."

"Your first act as this expedition's leader," Grant said to Casey, "is to ban all pre-dawn wake-up calls."

Grant and the others dispersed and changed into more rugged clothing. They met up outside the tents.

Then, true to her word, Terri did make sure they had breakfast before she stepped away to change for the day's work. The fare was warmed up leftovers from the meal the early birds had eaten, but it was still bacon, biscuits, and gravy. Grant and Casey dug in. Priya picked at the biscuit a bit, left the table, and returned with a banana and an orange.

"I should have mentioned that I'm a vegan before we left," she said.

Grant had never understood anyone's ability to turn down a cheeseburger, but wasn't about to start that conversation with Priya right now.

"That won't be a problem," Casey said.

Terri returned to the tent. She wore a set of Neoborax coveralls. The utility belt around her waist hosted a pair of work gloves, a canteen, and a knife big enough to intimidate a grizzly bear.

"Terri," Casey said, "you can make sure there's a vegetarian option at each meal?"

"Vegan," Priya corrected.

"Vegan," Casey echoed.

"Absolutely," Terri said.

Grant decided he was going to enjoy this dig. He'd have the freedom to poke around at his own speed, get first pick on what to bring back to the university, and above all, eat well while doing it. This trip was going to be fantastic.

As Grant finished the remains of his biscuit, he turned to Terri. "Can I see the fossils you've unearthed so far?"

"As soon as you're finished eating."

"Finished eating" was a phrase Grant rarely admitted to. He'd been mulling over the need for a second biscuit before the strenuous day ahead. But there was more food where this food came from. He could wait until lunch.

Grant wiped his mouth with a napkin and looked at Priya and Casey. They'd finished a while ago. "You two are already done? You eat fast."

"We started with smaller portions," Priya said.

Okay, that stung, Grant thought. "Let's get to work."

Terri led them out of the tent. They passed by a supply tent. The open flap showed it was packed with materials and boxes. Grant liked the look of that. No driving hours each way for supplies they'd need.

A breeze blew back one corner of a tent flap to expose some crates with red triangular markings on the side. Casey grabbed Grant's arm and yanked him to a halt.

"Look at those," he said. "Those are crates of explosives."

Grant peered at them. "Are you sure?"

"I worked in coal mines. Yes, I'm sure."

Terri and Priya had kept walking. Casey called them back over.

"Terri, what's with the explosives?" he said. "We don't need those."

"Someone from the group added them to the list in case we needed to blast away rock for samples."

"That's not how geologic research is done," Casey said.

"And explosions turn priceless, intact fossils into worthless chips and pebbles," Grant said.

"Using any explosives is out of the question," Casey said, "and they need to be removed from the site today."

"As you wish," Terri said. "We just thought it better to have something you don't need out here than not have something you do need."

Terri led them away from the tent and stopped between two large crates at the canyon's edge. The canyon yawned a hundred yards wide here, with a sheer cliff in front of them. The other side of the canyon had a face just as vertical, but with an overhang so massive that Grant couldn't imagine how it hadn't collapsed. That made the canyon floor wider than the canyon opening, with a small river running down the center. Grant couldn't tell how large the river was because looking straight down at it gave him heart palpitations. The canyon had to be over three hundred feet deep. Grant stepped back behind one of the crates.

"Neoborax was surprised to find this canyon," Terri said. "It wasn't on any of the maps when they signed the exploratory lease. It's about ten miles long and it can get much narrower in other places. The whole thing runs north/south so both sides of the river get shadow and daylight as the sun crosses the sky. The river runs in from the cliff side at one end and out through a tunnel at the other. We don't know the source or where it empties to."

"It could be an underground aquifer at both ends," Casey said.

"Okay," Grant said as he looked around, "where are the fossils?"

Terri reached into one of the crates, pulled out a rock-climbing harness, and handed it to Grant.

Grant's gut sank under the leaden weight of dread. "Do I want to know what this is for?"

Terri pointed to a thick, white nylon rope anchored to the ground on the other side of the crates. The end of it snaked over the edge and down the cliff. "To keep you from falling off the rope as you rappel down into the canyon to look at the fossils."

CHAPTER SIX

Sweat broke out across Grant's forehead. He would have rather had a root canal than dangle from a rope hundreds of feet off a canyon floor. "I'm in no hurry. I'll just take the trail."

"There's no trail," Terri said. "The cliff is too sheer. And the rest of the canyon rim on this side has an extended overhang that makes even rappelling down impossible."

"Okay, then I'll settle for a helicopter."

"The canyon opening is too narrow and winding for that. Why do you think this place wasn't explored until now? Are you afraid of falling from the rope?"

"No, I'm afraid of the sudden stop at the bottom of the cliff."

"I guess you haven't rappelled before."

Grant thought back to the last time he'd rappelled. It had been down a granite cliff in South America with dinosaurs chasing him. "I've done it before, but the inspiration to get me to do it was extreme. And just because I lived through something once doesn't mean I'll do it again."

Casey rested a hand on his shoulder. "Relax. Everyone else has been getting up and down from there safely. So will you."

Priya reached past him and grabbed the harness. "I don't know about you, but I did not come all this way to stand around up here."

Casey whispered in his ear. "You don't want her to make you look bad, do you?"

"She'd be joining a pretty long list." But Grant knew that his fossils were at the bottom of the canyon, and this was the only way down.

Terri grabbed a harness from the crate and gave everyone rudimentary instructions on how to hookup and descend. The group donned harnesses and heavy gloves.

"I'll go first," Terri said, "and help you transition to the second rope halfway down."

"Transition?" Grant said. "Like get off one and onto another?"

"Just like that."

"I keep trying to think of a way to make this day worse, but you keep beating me to it."

Terri clipped herself into the heavy nylon rope and disappeared over the edge. A minute or two later, she called up for the next person to follow.

"Ladies first?" Grant said to Priya.

Priya rolled her eyes. She stepped up, hooked in, and backed over to the edge. Then she hopped out into space with no more concern than if she'd been stepping into an elevator. She slid down the rope and vanished.

"It's so easy, an anthropology professor can do it," Casey said.

That didn't make Grant feel any safer.

The big rope stopped wiggling and Terri shouted for the next person to go.

"You're next," Casey said. "Otherwise, I'm afraid if you're the last one left up here, you won't go."

"That would be a distinct possibility."

Grant hooked up to the line and backed over to the edge. One glance over his shoulder was all it took to start his head reeling. His heart began to hammer in his chest. He turned back around and pressed his glasses tighter to his face.

Then he focused on his feet. A few inches at a time, he let the rope pass through his gloved hands and leaned out over the edge. Then with his feet flat against the sandstone cliff, he started to walk down.

"Doing great!" Casey said.

Grant looked up to see the geology professor's smiling face staring down at him. "I don't need an audience for this performance."

"You got it!" Casey backed away and all Grant could see was the solid blue desert sky. He shifted his focus back to the rocks and his feet as he walked down the cliff.

"You can push out and drop several yards at a time," Terri called up. There was no missing the barely disguised frustration in her voice.

Grant thought he was more likely to enter an alligator pit than to follow her recommendation. He continued his slow descent.

Halfway down, he stepped back with his right foot and rested against a protruding rock. Just as Grant sighed over having an easier foothold, the rock broke free. It tumbled down and left Grant with no grip. He clamped his hands on the rope in panic as he dropped and then swung sideways into the cliff. He slammed the earth shoulder-first and sent a shower of sandy soil across his face and into his mouth. Dust turned his view through his glasses into a rose-tinged haze.

From below came the crack of the falling rock hitting stone and breaking.

"Hey, watch what you're doing up there!" Terri said. "There's people down below you."

Grant wanted to tell her she was lucky only the rock had fallen and not him along with it. But fear had sucked the moisture from his mouth and left his throat too dry to say anything. He twisted himself back around so his feet were again against the cliff. He spat some dirt from his lips and continued down.

A few minutes later, his burning arm and leg muscles cheered with relief as he landed on the narrow ledge where Terri had been waiting. He exhaled so hard that he sent up a cloud of dust from the cliff face.

"That took long enough," Terri said.

"I was cherishing the moment."

Terri grabbed the back of his belt. "Switch ropes."

Grant did not want to look down to the canyon floor. He focused on swapping the ropes in his climbing harness. "Is Priya off the second rope?"

"A long time ago. Maybe you can get down there before sunset?"

"I'll do my best."

Grant leaned back and began his second descent. Terri shouted for Casey to start down from the canyon rim. Then she called again. Grant paused and looked up the cliff. Casey finally peered down, then backed himself over the edge.

Grant continued down. His shoulder was beginning to throb from where he'd slammed it into the cliff. The climbing harness was seriously chafing him where his stomach rolled over it. There wasn't a muscle in his body that was enjoying this little jaunt. He knew this would be easier if he was at least a dozen pounds lighter.

"As soon as I get back from this trip," he said to himself, "I am totally getting back into shape." He blew a drop of sweat off the tip of his nose. "Or more accurately into shape for the first time."

His feet passed some scrubby looking plants. That told him he was getting closer to the bottom where the moisture from the stream could support more plant life. A quick glance over his shoulder confirmed he was about eight feet up. In his relief, he dropped the last few feet so quickly the rope threatened to burn his hand through the gloves. His soles touched the canyon floor and he stifled a shout of joy. Grant unhooked the rope from his harness and stepped away on wobbly legs.

The canyon floor was a flurry of activity, with a swarm of people arranging equipment and moving boxes around. A camp of big canvas tents stood in a cleared spot halfway between the cliff face and the shallow river that ran down the canyon center.

The diversity of the plants in this desert canyon amazed him. The canyon's isolated ecosystem managed to support a healthy selection of trees and bushes. A denser thicket of plant life grew along the riverbanks.

Halfway up, Casey landed on the ledge beside Terri. She grabbed his waist and they began working to switch the ropes.

Suddenly, the top of the cliff exploded in an enormous fireball.

CHAPTER SEVEN

A bright orange sphere of fire erupted from the canyon rim. What sounded like a sonic boom cracked through the air and sent a shudder through the cliff. A cloud of earth and dust burst across the sky. Dark flecks in the cloud grew larger. Grant realized it was about to rain rocks.

A desperate look around the canyon area revealed no overhead cover. Near his feet, a scrubby pine grew about three feet tall with a crown of sparse branches. Grant dove beneath its illusion of protection and covered his head and neck with his arms.

A torrent of rocks rained on the canyon floor, some straight down, some bouncing off the cliff face. Metal crunched and canvas ripped as the shower of stones struck the work area. People cried out in pain and fear. Rocks peppered Grant along his arms and back. Each felt like it had been fired from a gun.

To his left something that made a sound like the slither of a giant snake hissed to the ground. When the shotgun-like assault of stones ceased, Grant opened one eye to see what lay beside him. He hoped like hell it wasn't a rattlesnake dislodged from the cliff.

It wasn't. It was something worse. The first of the climbing ropes lay in a pile at the base of the cliff. The hardware that had secured it to the canyon rim was still attached.

Grant waved away the airborne dust to see up the cliff. The edge of the canyon rim where the rope had been was now a jagged mess. The good news was the second rope was still in place, and somehow Terri and Casey had clung to the canyon wall at the midpoint and not plunged down along with the rope.

"Casey!" Grant called up. "You okay?"

Casey turned his head ever so slightly, just enough so he didn't shout back into the wall. "Seems so."

Terri checked the pitons that held the remaining rope in place. "These are secure. We're coming down."

Grant stepped away from the rope to give them space. As he dusted the dirt from his clothes he looked about the work area for Priya. Downslope, she knelt by the river, splashing water on her face. He was glad she hadn't been injured.

Grant counted over a dozen people checking themselves and the equipment around the site. Others hadn't been so lucky. One dust-coated man lay under a boulder about seven feet across. Rocks had turned canvas shade covers into a facsimile of Swiss cheese. A lot of the equipment looked like it had been damaged, some more severely than others.

Grant gave all the equipment a double-take. This wasn't the kind of stuff he'd seen at scientific digs. There were digging tools and the like, but they were industrial, what people use to excavate for a foundation, not to sample strata or extract hundred-million-year-old fossils from the ground.

Casey made it to the bottom of the rope and unhooked. Terri came down a moment later. Grant went over to them.

"Terri, what the hell just happened?" Grant said.

"I think I can answer that," Casey said. "All those improperly stored explosives detonated."

Terri bristled. "Those were stored by the book. There's no way they could have spontaneously blown up."

"Then by an amazing coincidence," Grant said, "a meteor must have hit the camp right in the explosives tent."

Anger flashed in Terri's eyes. "Your sarcasm is zero help here."

Casey reached down and picked up one end of the first rappelling rope. "This is going to be a problem. Who's up there to hook us up another rope?"

"There are several team members still in camp. Or at least there were. Honestly, if none of them have radioed down to check on us…"

Her voice trailed off and Grant didn't like the sentence she refused to finish. Terri took a walkie talkie from her belt and tried to raise anyone in camp. She got no answer.

Terri grimaced. "Everyone up there is either dead or too badly injured to help us out. This whole job just went straight to hell."

"First thing is to call in medical help," Casey said.

Priya stepped up beside Grant and Casey. "I've worked in canyons like this before. They are so deep and narrow that even satellite phones don't work."

"Even if they did," Terri said, "mine is in pieces up in the camp."

"As the expedition's leader," Casey said, "I'm calling this whole goat rope to a halt."

Terri rolled her eyes. Her cheery tour guide façade dropped like a used Halloween mask. In its place was an angry, frustrated woman. "News flash, Professor. You are not, and never were the leader here. Now that this whole operation has gone sideways, I don't have the time to keep pretending that you are."

"What are you talking about?" Casey said. "I have a contract stating that I'm to run this dig."

"Have your lawyer call ours on that. What you're really here for is to put your name on the permits so they'd be approved and we could work out here without anyone from the government breathing down our necks."

Casey looked stunned.

Grant couldn't believe what he was hearing. "That can't be true."

"Look around, Professor. Does any of this look like a science dig is going on? So for now, you three shut up and stay out of our way. I told Neoborax to keep you away from the site and have you check in remotely. But no, they wouldn't do that. Now this is screwed up six ways from Sunday and I need to babysit you three on top of it. Or the three of you can help clear that rockfall."

"We're scientists," Grant said. "Our forte is more making and testing hypotheses."

"I need to see what we can salvage." Terri stomped over to where the rest of the crew were recovering from the rocky hailstorm. Casey looked crestfallen and humiliated.

Grant put a hand on Casey's shoulder. "You couldn't know what they were up to. Wasn't Dean Malley the one who set all this up?"

"Yes," Casey said, "but he would never agree to a sham dig if he knew, no matter how much money the college was offered."

"I agree," Priya said. "In fact, upper management in Neoborax might not even know what Terri and this crew are up to."

"Well, I say first things first and that means getting the hell out of here." Grant led the others over to where Terri was rolling up a shredded canvas cover. She ignored him.

"Let's talk about this situation," Grant said. "What is it you are looking for here if it isn't fossils?"

"Uranium deposits. Big ones. Why do you think we needed the geologist for a cover story? Can you imagine the public backlash if we had open hearings about starting a uranium mine?"

"You'll still need to deal with those hearings to actually open a mine," Casey said.

"Sure, after we have a proven, exploitable vein and months to do the right political maneuvering."

"You mean bribing," Grant said.

"You'd be surprised how cheaply people sell out."

"I'm mad about being used," Casey said, "but none of this is my fight. Get us up to the canyon rim. We'll see if there's anyone alive or any vehicles available to get us back to civilization. We won't breathe a word of this to anyone, except Neoborax so they can start a relief mission for everyone else."

"There's no way back up there except for a free climb." She looked at Grant's belly. "Not sure all of you are up for that. For now, all of you are staying here."

"You're going to put these two college professors here through this?" Casey said.

"No, you did that. You're the one who made me bring them along, remember?"

Casey looked guilty.

"Their fate is on you. Now stay out of the way. I have bigger problems to deal with than the three of you." Terri stomped off.

"Seems like we've had our stay with this group involuntarily extended," Grant said. "Neoborax's search for uranium trumps our personal lives."

"Could there be uranium out here?" Priya said.

"Oh, most definitely," Casey said. "There was a big uranium boom out in the desert west for many years. In fact, there's even an old abandoned uranium mine in the wall of the Grand Canyon.

We've been importing a lot of our uranium from overseas, so a new vein of it would be politically welcome."

"That's what Terri is counting on," Grant said, "whether the people who live here or those who preserve the environment are happy about it or not."

"Look," Casey said, "I'm really sorry I got either of you involved with this at all."

"On the bright side," Priya said, "at least we were down here when the camp exploded."

"I feel better already," Grant said.

CHAPTER EIGHT

Terri Nagle was pissed as hell.

What she loved to do was blast holes in the ground. The bigger, the better. Her pyrotechnic fascination had started at a young age with illegal fireworks. Feeding the hunger of this internal demon through her childhood had led her to detonating bigger and bigger displays. The culmination was to be the destruction of an old water tower outside her hometown to celebrate turning 18.

It hadn't gone as planned.

She'd hand-packed four charges, each with enough explosives to rip one of the legs right off the tower. She set them in place, lit the fuses and ran.

To this day she wasn't sure what went wrong, but only three charges went off. This sent the tower careening sideways instead of making the vertical collapse she'd planned. When the undamaged leg snapped, it catapulted the unexploded charge onto the roof of a nearby warehouse. At that moment the fuse decided to complete its mission and the charge exploded.

The resulting fireball was a glorious red and yellow sight to behold. A blast of overheated air swept past her and made her skin tingle. The entire experience sent a surge of adrenaline through her that she wished would never end. If she'd been unsure of her true calling before, she wasn't then. Blowing things up was her destiny. She'd been so captivated by this revelation that she hardly noticed the arrival of the police.

During her trial, her attorney told the jury how the warehouse had been a catastrophe waiting to happen, filled with highly flammable illegal Chinese imports. He also presented evidence that the natural gas safeties had been bypassed to save maintenance money. Her attorney also reminded everyone that Terri had been a minor at the time (true) and that she had no idea what she was really doing when she created and set the charges (totally untrue). A sympathetic group of twelve of her peers convicted her of a lesser misdemeanor charge and the judge admonished her that this experience should teach her a lesson.

Indeed it had. The lesson was she would need to find a legitimate way to blow things up. A career in mining had been a perfect fit.

She'd started at the bottom at Neoborax in the mining division, and rapidly worked her way up. The company had an appreciation for people who were not too shackled by safety regulations and were willing to cut corners that saved money or time. When a shady operation like this Desolation Canyon job came up, she was management's first choice to lead it.

It had promised to be a dream job. No oversight, no restrictions, and a crew of like-minded roughnecks and independent contractors unconnected to Neoborax. All she had to deal with would be some initial babysitting with a college professor, then it would be nothing but boom, boom, boom.

And then fifteen minutes ago an unplanned boom sent everything spinning out of control. One of the idiots on her crew must have stored some of the explosives improperly. Maybe that college professor Casey had been right after all.

Wiping out the base camp was going to be a problem. Losing the climbing ropes to get out of the canyon was going to be a bigger problem. The good news was Neoborax would send someone in to find them once they realized contact had been lost. Until then, she could go back to the boom, boom, boom. No point just sitting around down here.

Her only question was how much booming she could do. They hadn't transferred everything to the canyon floor yet, and falling rock had damaged some of the equipment they did have. As she stood amidst what was left of the canyon worksite, her crew lead, Karl Kraus, came up beside her. The tall, thin man had snow-white hair and piercing blue eyes. Dust coated his face and rolling beads of sweat had run tracks through it down the side of his face.

"We have three dead," Kraus said, "and one man with a leg so smashed it needs to be amputated. A tourniquet is all that's keeping him alive."

That wasn't the update Terri was looking for. "Equipment?"

"We lucked out and none of the gas-powered generators or compressors were hit."

"Explosives?"

"They dodged the boulders, or you sure as hell would have heard it. Everything we had down here made it okay."

"Then let's get back to work."

Kraus looked incredulous. "Are you kidding? How about getting out of here?"

"Neoborax will come for us. But until they do..."

She looked around the worksite until she spied Sanjay, a wiry little man with dark skin and an oversized nose. She remembered how desperate he'd been to get hired for this job because he needed to send his pay to support his family in Nepal. She called him over.

He sprinted over to Terri with a big smile on his face. "Yes, ma'am."

"You helped Johnson set up those climbing ropes, right?"

Sanjay's look turned nervous. "Yes, but he did most of the work."

"Well, I saw him crushed by a boulder so you just got promoted to senior cliff climber. Go scale that cliff, run us a new line from the top, and then see if anything useful survived the blast."

Sanjay looked about to object. Terri delivered a glare so intense it could have started a fire.

"Yes," Sanjay said, "Yes, ma'am."

He headed for where the rappelling rope hung on the cliff. This time he wasn't sprinting.

"Sanjay isn't an experienced enough climber to do a free climb like that," Kraus said.

"He's from Nepal. Isn't climbing mountains like the national pastime or something? He'll be fine."

Moments later, there was movement on the cliff side. Sanjay ratcheted himself up the remaining rappelling rope. He made it to the ledge and took a break.

Terri exhaled in relief. She hoped she'd start waking from this nightmare now. Sanjay was going to get back to the canyon rim, then he was going to find a working radio, and then Neoborax would be sending help sooner rather than later. While that was going on, she'd keep blasting this canyon and find that vein of uranium.

Sanjay shook out his arms, studied the newly rearranged cliff face, and then began to climb. Hand over hand, and foot over foot, he inched his way up the sandstone wall. The rope that had dropped from the canyon rim was attached to his belt and played out behind him like a ridiculously long tail. He was so far away that Terri couldn't make out the tiny outcroppings and exposed rocks he was using as hand and footholds. That made it seem like he was Spider-man, just sticking to the wall.

A short distance up, he paused and drove a steel piton into the stone. When he was finished, he hooked a carabiner to the wedge and looped the rope through it. Then after a couple of deep breaths, he continued his climb.

"I'll be damned," Kraus said.

Kraus and Terri weren't the only ones who were interested in Sanjay's cliff-scaling heroics. The rest of the Neoborax team had stopped what they were doing, found a place with a clear line of sight, and were watching Sanjay climb. Everyone had to know their rapid rescue depended on Sanjay's success. Several shouted out encouragement as the little man worked his way up.

Sanjay shot a glance and a quick smile over one shoulder and then continued his climb. With great care, he picked his way up the cliff face, somehow finding purchase with hands and feet with each movement.

At the cliff's base, a swell of audible encouragement rose from the workers. The air seemed thick with hope and anticipation. Terri imagined the intensity of the emotions boosting Sanjay higher up the rock face.

"That guy is going to surprise me and get this job done," Kraus said.

At three-quarters of the way up, Sanjay wedged himself into a crevice in the wall. After a pause for a few deep breaths, he held a piton against the rock with his left hand. Then he gripped his hammer in his right, swung it, and struck the piton head.

Metal clanged on metal. Whatever tenuous surface tension kept the weakened cliff face together shattered. The earth all around

Sanjay dropped like a theater curtain. For a split second he seemed to stay suspended in mid-air.

Then Sanjay screamed and fell backward. His body tumbled down the cliff, bouncing in and out of the growing avalanche of debris. The climbing rope was still attached to him and it pulled each piton from the cliff as it passed, like a doctor pulling stitches from a patient.

Sanjay hit the midpoint ledge and cartwheeled further away from the cliff. The sandstone cascade followed him down and swept the remaining climbing gear from the cliff face.

Freefalling rock hurtled toward the workers closest to the cliff. Men bolted for safety. A split-second later, stone and sand thundered to the ground right where they'd been standing. A cloud of dust rolled away from the cliff, blew past Terri, and then settled on the plants all around her.

Terri cursed as she spat the dust from her lips. The new avalanche had damaged even more equipment. Worse yet, now both climbing ropes lay in tangled messes around Sanjay's broken body. Workers moaned in despair.

Terri cursed under her breath. *That idiot Sanjay just screwed up the easy route out of here*, she thought.

CHAPTER NINE

Down at the riverbed, Grant's hopes for an early release from Desolation Canyon had risen as he, Casey, and Priya had watched the young Neoborax employee scale the cliff face with the apparent ease of a lizard up a screen door. Then those hopes were extinguished as the poor man plummeted from the cliff in a dusty hail of sandstone. Thankfully, the sight of his impact with the ground had been shielded by some vegetation, but the awful, crunching sound of it hadn't been.

"Dear God," Priya whispered.

"I could have warned them not to try and send someone up that sandstone cliff," Casey said. "The impact of that blast would have made the whole formation unstable."

"They're miners," Grant said. "You can bet that Terri knew that as well as you do. I've had the misfortune of working with people like her before."

"I thought people like that were just characters in those little monster books you write," Priya said.

"I wish they were."

"Casey, do you think someone like that will actually let us get out of this alive?" Priya said.

"She might," Casey said. "Here's how these things work. Everyone at Neoborax will lie. They will claim the uranium find was accidental while we were looking for fossils. If we try and tell the truth, they will paint us as opportunists trying to get a cut of the mining profits. Their word against ours and you can be damn sure they won't leave us any evidence to back up our side of the story."

"I was worried about being left for dead down here," Grant said. "I'll take public humiliation and ridicule over that any day."

"That said," Casey said, "the more we stay out of the way and fade into the background, the better off we'll be."

"I think I have found something to keep me busy while we stay out of their way." Priya took a rock from one pocket. It was eight inches long and about half as wide. One end came to a rudimentary point.

Grant looked at the unremarkable rock, and then looked back at Priya.

"Don't you see what this is?" Priya said.

"All rocks that aren't fossilized animal remains look the same to me," Grant said.

Priya sighed and flipped the rock around in her hand. She closed her fingers around it and now it was obvious that a grip had been chiseled into the stone. The creator could hold it with the pointy end facing down. In this orientation, that pointy end suddenly looked a lot more unnatural.

"This is a hand ax," Priya said.

"Can you chisel us a stairway out of here with it?" Grant said.

Priya sighed like she was speaking to a child. "This was a common tool among early indigenous peoples in the Southwest. This larger, harder stone was used to chip away and sharpen arrowheads."

"How old do you think that is?" Casey said.

"It might be over two thousand years old." She turned to Grant. "Brand new by the standards you dinosaur diggers use, but older than most tribes we get to study in this area."

"Where did you find it?" Casey said.

"Lying beside the riverbed. It must have been scoured away or washed down from upstream. This is a major find in an area no one has excavated before."

"Well, then it ended up being a lucky thing that you were held against your will by a group of duplicitous, exploitive miners," Grant said. "Who would have guessed?"

"I'm going back to the river. If this ax washed up there, lighter artifacts might have as well."

"I'm going to keep an eye on whatever mining exploration they're doing," Casey said.

"I'll find a shady spot here," Grant said. "And conserve energy for the adventures that lay ahead of us."

The others moved off and Grant walked midway between the cliff and the river. Fear of pulverization meant he was in no hurry to get too close to the cliff. Luckily, he found a spot beneath a tree where several small boulders from a previous calamity had taken up residence. The upright L-shaped one of them looked like a solid, but quite serviceable chair.

Grant made his way to it and took a seat. It was hard, but being in the shade had kept it cool, so that part of the experience was pleasant. He leaned back and wondered if there was any chance this was an elaborate practical joke Casey had engineered.

He looked over at the boulder beside his barely-comfortable chair. A pattern on the side of it immediately caught his paleontologist's eye. He went over to the rock and bent down beside it.

He first thought his eyes were playing tricks on him, working hand in hand with his wishful thinking. But that was not true. When this boulder had calved itself from the cliff side, it had exposed a beautiful fossil skull. It was common for pressure over the centuries to compress and distort larger bones like these, but this specimen was in outstanding condition. The bird-like skull was larger than a man's, with a mouth full of sharp, shredding teeth and a set of forward-looking eyes for the binocular vision a predator required.

Given their location and the age of the sediments around him, Grant didn't need to unearth any more of this skull to make an identification. This was a *Coelophysis*. If the rest of the body had still been attached, the creature would have been about ten feet long, with short forelimbs and powerful rear legs. The extended, slender tail was believed to be used primarily for balance as the predator ran down its hapless prey. These things had been lethal hunters during the Triassic period.

Grant's reason for embarking on this expedition-turned-disaster had been to bring back fossils. Even if the only one he brought back was this one, that would be fantastic. This kind of currency might buy his silence about being brought here under false pretenses. Of course, he'd still anonymously tip someone off about illegal mining. He did have ethics.

Grant gave the fossilized skull a pat. "Say, Coelophysis, old pal. Want to hear a story about a college professor who gets trapped in a canyon?"

Grant hoped the real-life version of the story would wrap up with a happy ending.

CHAPTER TEN

Grant walked upstream a bit. While he would not have minded spending more time with Priya, he would have very much minded bending over to sift through riverbed looking for arrowheads and pottery shards. He knew anthropology was an important field of study and he completely respected the skill those experts had at teasing a lot of information from the smallest finds. But seriously, compared to finding fossils like the *Coelophysis* skull he'd discovered? Talk about underwhelming.

Making his way up the narrow, rocky riverbank, he rounded a bend that gave him a clear view of the north end of the canyon. In the distance a spring-fed waterfall exited a hole on the upper canyon wall to feed the river. Torrents of white water hammered a collection of rocks at the waterfall's base.

At least we won't die of dehydration down here, he thought.

He paused at a calmer section of the river. Water hyacinth grew along the edge, but they were much larger than any he'd ever seen, with leaves several feet wide. He knelt and examined one more closely. The air bladder keeping it at the surface stretched over a foot across. The structure of the leaf was oversized and simple.

In the same way he made no claim to being an anthropologist, he also wasn't a biologist. But he'd seen enough plant fossils to recognize an archaic bit of flora when he saw it in green instead of some variation of brown. He'd taught hours of lectures on extinct plants and their evolution into current species. This hyacinth was about as modern as a diplodocus.

He checked the other plants around the shore. He'd been on enough digs in the American Southwest to recognize them as common species for the area.

The giant hyacinth was quite a survivor. Over the course of multiple mass extinctions, it had endured in this tiny pocket of green in the middle of a desert. Newer species had joined it here, blown in by the wind, washed in by rain, or maybe carried in by birds. But this tough little species, with its much more rudimentary photosynthetic and cellular structure, had stood its ground and refused to be crowded out.

Grant gave a hyacinth leaf a stroke. "Way to go, kid. Any other blasts from the past living down here you want to direct me to?"

The plant, understandably, did not answer.

He immediately worried that his contact with it might upset whatever delicate equilibrium it maintained with this isolated environment. That would be just his luck. Instead of bringing back a living sample, he'd send the entire species the way of the passenger pigeon.

He went down to the stream and built a cairn of rocks along the bank. This would give him a marker to come back to when he did need to get a sample of that plant. Then he started walking back downstream.

He soon saw Priya and Casey chatting near the water's edge south of the encampment. Grant joined them.

"What a coincidence meeting you two out here in the desert," Grant said. "Find anything interesting, Priya?"

"Two pieces that might have been arrowheads," Priya said, "but water has made them too smooth to be sure."

"And you, Casey?"

"I've been watching them work. They're sampling a specific stratum all along the cliff. They obviously know where the uranium will be, if it's there at all."

Grant waited for the question he considered inevitable. It didn't come.

"Are you going to ask me if *I* found anything interesting?"

"Gee, Grant," Casey said. "Did you find anything interesting?"

"So glad you asked. I found an excellent fossilized skull of a *Coelophysis*."

That elicited two blank stares.

"Assume if it wasn't in a *Jurassic Park* movie," Casey said, "we don't know one dinosaur from the next."

"This was a nasty predator from the Triassic. A lean, mean eating machine. They've been found in this area and I think the skull will be one of the best examples. But there's more."

"More exciting than finding a fossil?" Priya said.

Grant ignored the sarcastic tone of her question. "Oh, yeah. There are primitive water hyacinths growing here, a species with attributes that went extinct a long time ago. This isolated place has sheltered them for who-knows-how-many million years."

Neither of the two looked excited about his discovery.

"You people don't appreciate this discovery at all," Grant said.

"You found a plant," Priya said. "I may have discovered a civilization."

"Okay, well I also saw the source of this river," Grant said, "if either of you think that's interesting. It's a waterfall at the north end of the canyon."

"That *is* more interesting," Casey said.

"I've seen in caves where an underground stream appears at one end and then disappears at the other end," Grant said. "But I've never seen a surface river do that the way this one does."

"There are examples around the world," Casey said. "But they're rare. My guess is that an underground river scoured away the weaker upper strata millions of years ago and created this canyon."

"The opportunity to get year-round access to fresh water would be the first thing to attract a native tribe to the area," Priya said. "Between cultivating the canyon floor and hunting above the rim, a fairly large group could thrive here."

From up the canyon came a chorus of men shouting "Fire in the hole!" followed by a deep boom. The ground vibrated beneath Grant's feet. A puff of sand-colored smoke billowed out from the canyon wall.

"Being trapped here isn't slowing them down any," Casey said. "They must have a tight deadline."

"Made tighter by the potential of someone other than Neoborax looking for us when we don't check in with our families," Priya said.

"My wife will request the governor send out the Utah National Guard to rescue me," Casey said.

"My ex-wife has an embalmer on retainer," Grant said, "hoping for an occasion like this."

"We might want to move a bit further downstream," Casey said. "Blasting around unstable cliff walls is asking for trouble. We saw what happened to the poor climber."

Grant did not need to be asked twice. He wheeled around and began to move downstream.

Casey did not follow. "You know, I'll hang back and keep an eye on what they're doing. I don't trust them to not make things worse."

"So far," Grant said, "Terri has excelled at doing that."

CHAPTER ELEVEN

Priya and Grant began to pick their way downstream as Casey returned to the worksite. The silence between them made Grant uncomfortable. He struggled to come up with some clever small talk.

Priya broke the silence first. "You have to question your academic career choice sometimes, right?"

If Priya's idea of small talk was to attack Grant's career, the previous silence suddenly didn't seem so unbearable.

"What do you mean?" he said.

"Well, paleontologists can never really answer a question. You all just study fragments and fossils and then take a guess at an extinct animal's properties, followed by an even wilder guess at its behavior. But since you'll never see an extinct animal, you'll never know if you were correct."

Grant could have made a short list of the supposedly "extinct" animals he'd encountered over the last years, but decided that might make him sound a little crazy. "With the best evidence, I think we can feel confident in our hypotheses."

"But they seem to always be changing. Dinosaurs don't have feathers, and then do. Dinosaurs were slow and plodding, now they were quick and nimble. Then take the dinosaurs with the…" Priya made a motion with one hand as if stroking a large horn protruding from the top of her head.

"Head crests," Grant volunteered, as he stepped around a few larger stones on the riverbank.

"Yes, head crests. You people don't even know what those features were for."

Grant felt like he was donning armor and rising to fight in defense of his profession. "It's true that our interpretations change over time as we discover more evidence. But that's part of what makes it exciting. You never know if the fossil you just cleaned will be the one that overturns decades of conventional wisdom."

Priya snapped a protruding branch to make her passage easier. "And then next week, someone else does the same to you."

Grant was done playing defense on this one. "You do the same things with your pottery fragments and animal bones you dig up, trying to piece together the lives of tribes so long-lost that you have to make up names for them."

Priya dismissed him with a wave of her hand. "That is a fraction of my research. Most of my work is around current indigenous peoples. By studying what makes these simple societies work, I hope to diagnose what is dysfunctional in our complex ones."

Grant's personal theory was that studying a tribe in the Amazon was as valuable to helping a modern society as studying a Ford Model T would be in diagnosing a Tesla Model S. But they might be in this canyon for a while and this was no time to turn one of the two friendly faces down here into an enemy. "Even with our different focuses in studies, I think we can both agree to swear off attending any future geological digs if they're going to end up like this one."

Priya smiled, which Grant decided to take as an apology for being so dismissive of paleontology, whether that was its meaning or not. "Yes, Casey has gotten us into a predicament."

They'd been skirting the river for a while to keep from having to bushwhack through the plant life along the riverbank. But ahead on the right appeared what looked like a trail that led away from the river and toward the cliffs. Grasses had grown in along the edges, but a sandy stripe down the middle still led away from the water.

"An animal trail," Grant said.

"Made by animals we have yet to see?" Priya said.

"Nothing would spook them faster than a gang of strange bipeds blowing up the canyon walls," Grant said.

Grant led Priya up the trail. Halfway to the cliff, they came across a ring of flat stones a few feet across. Within it, nothing sprouted in the bare, sandy soil. Two tall palms grew on each side. They bent inward about fifteen feet up and crossed each other.

Priya gasped and knelt beside it. She ran a finger across the stones. "Look at this! You may not recognize a hand axe, but even you can tell this was made by humans. This is proof-positive that a native culture was once here."

"Unless Neoborax guys made it."

"Have you seen any footprints along this trail? Do you see how the edges are overgrown but the center is not? This arrangement has been here a while, and we may be the first to see it in centuries. I'm coming back later to take extensive notes on this find."

Priya gave the find the same look a kid gives a birthday present, and then continued up the trail. Grant followed, still missing how a ring of rocks could be that exciting.

At the base of the cliff, in the shadow of the cliffside overhang, the trail dead-ended.

"This is odd," Grant said. "Animals wouldn't come this way all the time if there wasn't something worthwhile at this destination."

He checked the wall for a natural salt lick and found nothing. The slight uphill angle of the jaunt had left him breathless, the absence of some kind of worthwhile destination disheartened. He slumped down on a stone by the canyon wall, mopped his brow, and then cleaned his dusty glasses.

"Do you see what you're sitting on?" Priya said.

"My well-cushioned butt?"

"No, get up."

Grant put his glasses back on, stood, and turned around. Even through clean lenses, the rock still looked like a rock, the surface smoothed by weather, with a slight dip to the right. "I still don't see it."

"For someone who studies things turned to stone, you are kind of obtuse."

Priya went to the rock, bent down, and swept the lighter sand away from the top. She exposed a flat surface about a foot and a half wide and three feet across. The rock at both ends met at an unnatural 90-degree angle. Once cleared of the sand, it was obvious that the feature was manmade.

Priya stood in front of the stone, and set her right foot into the little dip. It was a near perfect fit.

"This is a step," she said. "Carved right into the cliff. The Anasazi were masters at this."

"Looks more like a seat, validating my use of it."

Priya made a frustrated growl. She snapped a leafy branch off a nearby tree. Using it, she swept and picked at the area behind and to the left of the step. Falling sand and stone exposed parts of a stairway that turned and followed the cliff face upward.

She turned back to Grant with a satisfied smile on her face. "See, it's a stairway, the kind desert dwellers made to get to their villages."

Grant looked up at the wide, overhanging rim of the canyon. "Unless they could hang upside down, no stairway would get them to the rim from here."

"They didn't live on the rim." Priya jogged past Grant, stopped, and examined the overhang above them. She took out her phone.

"There's still no signal here," Grant said. "I checked."

Priya ignored him and aimed her phone at the overhang. She took a few pictures, then went back to Grant.

"Look here." She called up one of the pictures, then enlarged it to maximum. It was hard for Grant to see, but it seemed like there was a square shape built into the cliff within the overhang's shadow.

"Is that really some kind of building up there?"

"Absolutely. Adobe cliff structures like that were how the Anasazi people lived in canyons like these in Colorado for a while until 1100 AD."

"They were humans, not cliff swallows. There are way easier places to build a home than on a vertical surface."

"That is true, and that's why the Anasazi are such a mystery. Why did they live in a place like that, and why after the relatively short period of time of several generations did they disappear?"

"What do you mean disappear?"

"The dwellings were completely abandoned. When they were re-discovered in 1888, useful artifacts that a migrating tribe would take with them were still in place. None of the local tribal histories include stories of ancestors migrating from cliff side dwellings, so it doesn't seem like these people were the predecessors of a more modern tribe. They just evaporated."

"Fantastic. I was afraid that the only scary thing in the canyon would be mining explosions. I feel much better adding mysterious mass deaths."

Priya gave the dwellings a wistful look. "Imagine what we could discover up there."

"Let me see. We could discover the sensation of falling off a cliff. We could discover that thousand-year-old adobe can no longer support the weight of a human being. We could discover that a hundred generations of rattlesnakes took over when the humans departed. I'm happy making none of those discoveries."

"Don't be silly. Native American children used to scamper up and down these steps for centuries."

"And I'm so out of practice scampering that I've completely forgotten how to do it."

"Fine. I was giving you the benefit of the doubt being scared to rappel down here. But not climbing steps? Seriously? I'll just go myself."

Grant looked up the sheer face of the cliff. The cliffside village looked about ten thousand feet away, though he knew it was only a fraction of that distance. His still twitchy heart muscle said to forget the climb. His sore legs agreed. His bulging stomach reminded him that his center of gravity was too high to be attempting such a balancing act.

But his pride, so frequently swallowed that it had a sleeping cot in his stomach, stirred itself to life. If this petite anthropologist was ready to scale the cliff, he couldn't just sit down here and watch. Besides, this might be the pivot point where she noticed something good about him.

"Okay," he said. "Up we go. If we can find the steps."

Priya handed him the branch. "Start sweeping."

CHAPTER TWELVE

Grant sighed and went to work sweeping as Priya searched for another branch suitable for use as a broom. Most of what covered the staircase was dust and sand that had trickled down over the last thousand years. A few newer and larger rocks bore witness to the recent rounds of explosive activity Terri and her crew had been doing.

Priya returned with a leafy branch and went to work right behind Grant. The narrowness of the steps and the relatively short riser distance, coupled with a lack of anything resembling a handrail made Grant even more nervous the higher they climbed.

"These steps aren't even wide enough for one person," he said, "let alone having people pass in opposite directions."

"Not wide enough for a modern person, but they must have been fine for the people who lived here. They had to have been smaller than our modern average person. See, you hypothesize things based on the fossils you unearth, we do the same from what we find."

Grant looked down over the side of the steps to the canyon floor far below. "If we root around down there, I'll bet we find a big pile of broken bones, leading me to hypothesize that these people should have invented the banister."

Grant managed the rest of the climb by focusing on his feet and the next step, working very hard to not look down at the canyon floor again. A harrowing eternity later, he set foot onto a kind of patio about five feet square. At the other side, a final set of steps led up to where they had seen the cliff face building, though it wasn't visible from the vantage point of the patio. With a sigh of relief, he stepped over to the cliff wall and rested against it. Sweat rolled down his face and his breathing was beyond labored.

Priya zipped by him for the far end of the patio, displaying an annoying lack of physical exhaustion. She bent and swept the dirt from the floor.

"I was going to clear away all that." Grant exhaled hard. "But didn't want to steal the experience from you."

"I'm going to surmise that this was a lookout post," Priya said as she swept. "An outpost separate from the rest of the community where one person could keep a watch on the only entrance to the village."

Grant eased himself away from the canyon wall. "Defending this place would be easy. Anyone climbing those steps would be in no condition for a fight by the time they made it up here."

"That is one theory about why people built communities like this, defense against marauding tribes."

"If I'm part of a marauding tribe," Grant said, "I'm not climbing all the way down into the canyon so that I can climb all the way back up those steps just to attack this village. I'd rather hunt my own bison. It would be safer."

Grant wiped his brow and began to sweep the platform around the steps that led to it. Dirt obscured something chiseled into the platform edge facing that first step. He knelt and blew away the sand. His pulse went into overdrive.

The artwork was of a stick figure man, mouth open in a big O, arms extended out over his head. At his midsection, the head of a dinosaur had him in its jaws.

Marauding tribes might have been the least of these peoples' worries, he thought.

"I'm no anthropologist," Grant said, "but this looks like one of those warning stickers on electrical cabinets, except a dinosaur replaced the little lightning bolts."

Priya looked over her shoulder. "Ooh, that's an amazing find. And I'd say your assessment is correct. For a people without a language, this is a posted warning, either of danger beyond these steps, or the danger that may come up the steps."

"Why choose? Let's just say it's both. But that means the people here a thousand years ago were interacting with a species that should have been extinct."

Priya stifled a laugh. "Seriously? That drawing could represent a spirit creature or have some kind of allegorical meaning. Maybe it was some other animal, not a dinosaur. Early artwork isn't Renaissance master quality."

"That thing is reptilian," Grant said. "The elongated snout says alligator or crocodile, and there hasn't been anything like that within a thousand miles of here in millennia, let alone a thousand years ago when someone carved this happy little picture."

"I think that your study of dinosaurs has let you jump to a conclusion that this drawing has to be of a dinosaur. Take a deep breath and think about what you are saying. It's unrealistic to think dinosaurs could still be alive today."

From Grant's personal experience, it was not only realistic, it was dangerously irrefutable.

"Whatever that creature was," Priya said, "if it ever existed at all, it's long gone. No one in the crew has seen one, or they'd have never come back down into the canyon."

Grant had to admit she was right about that. It was damn hard to hide a dinosaur. He gestured to the final set of steps that led to the village. "This is your sandbox. After you."

Priya began to scale the final steps that led to the village. Grant hung back a few risers and then followed her up. He said to himself it was so he didn't bump into her, but not having her hear his labored breathing was high on the reasons list as well. When she got to the top, she gasped and paused. Then she stepped forward to make room for Grant.

When he stepped beside her, he understood her reaction. They stood on the edge of a wide plaza made of finished stone, as perfectly flat as any modern construction Grant had ever seen. The massive canyon overhang completely covered an entire village. Grant wondered if these ancient people had carved this opening out of the center of it to make the base and roof.

Along the cavern wall was a joined row of adobe rooms that looked like they'd been built into the wall. At least one larger building rose at the plaza's far end.

Grant took a step forward. Priya whacked him in the chest with her branch.

"Don't step there!" she said.

Grant looked down to see an array of petroglyphs carved in the plaza stones ahead of him. Sand obscured portions of them, but they were in the same crude style as the drawing of the man being eaten by a dinosaur.

"You climbed all the way up here," Grant said, "discovered this village, and you aren't going to check it out?"

"Are you kidding? Those petroglyphs carved down there are in an unknown style, making this village from an undiscovered people. I can't just wander into someplace that hasn't been disturbed in a thousand years with my only tool being a tree branch. We're going back to the main worksite and picking up some proper tools for this job and everything I'll need to document the village properly."

Grant looked up at the tons of rock that might fall on his head at any moment and kill him, then glanced down at the potential fall off the cliff that would do the exact same thing. He loved Priya's plan because it would get him the hell off this plaza and back somewhere closer to sea level. Then in the interest of minimizing any contamination of such a unique cultural artifact, he'd make a personal sacrifice and let Priya hike back up here alone to explore this collection of mud bricks.

"Good idea," he said. "I'll lead the way."

Without having to clear the steps as they did on the way up, and with gravity back on Grant's side, the trip back down was much quicker. With every step closer to the canyon floor, Grant had to work harder to suppress the urge to just jump the last bit of distance and get off these steps. But a vision of hobbling around on a twisted ankle kept him on the staircase and hugging the canyon wall. When he did set foot on solid ground, he almost cheered.

Priya joined him and they followed the trail back down to the riverbank. When they returned to the softer mud by the water, Priya laughed out loud.

Grant turned around to her. "What's so funny?"

"See, all this talk of dinosaurs has sent my imagination into overdrive. I saw the ground here and thought it looked like a dinosaur footprint."

Grant looked down to where she was pointing. An impression in the mud measured two feet long and a bit wider, with four equally long toes that ended in sharp claws. The sole of the footprint carried deep ridges instead of the flat surface left by human footprints. Grant's heart skipped a beat.

It looked like a dinosaur footprint to him, as well.

CHAPTER THIRTEEN

Brendan Ternan could kick himself for taking this screwed-up job in the desert.

He'd ignored all the red flags when he'd been recruited. The sponsoring company remained anonymous. His pay came from an obvious shell company and was in digital currency. Beefy security men had searched him for weapons and cell phones when he'd arrived at the camp on the canyon rim.

But the biggest red flag was his pay rate. He'd been fired from his last two mining gigs for drug use and safety violations, yet the mystery company had offered him twice the going rate for this job. No legit company does that. But that final, largest warning had also been the largest inducement. Brendan shouldered some staggering debts, and this payday promised to be enough to wipe them clean.

At first, he thought the job might be okay. The food was good, the equipment new, and the crew reminded him of himself. They were all people who worked best just a few feet outside the legal boundaries. His worries looked like they'd been unwarranted.

All that had changed today when the base camp blew up like a scene from an action movie. One boulder had flattened the guy standing beside him, missing Brendan by inches. The whole experience had been so incredible that Brendan had stood staring at the boulder for many moments with his mouth open. That kind of thing was way funnier when it happened in a Roadrunner cartoon.

The explosion's rain of rocks had crushed a lot of the camp at the cliff base. Within minutes, that bitch of a boss, Terri, was running around with Kraus trying to get business back to normal, but how could that happen when there was a pile of dead bodies at the base of the cliff?

Terri had gotten everyone back to work, as of course she would. They had just detonated a new set of charges and Brendan was cleaning up some of the aftermath.

He looked down and noticed that the boulder victim's blood, and maybe a bit more of him, still stippled his boots. The realization made Brendan queasy. He turned and headed for the river to wash the blood from his boots and the dirt from his hands and face. Then he was going to take some personal time and evaluate the decisions that had left him trapped at the bottom of a canyon in the middle of nowhere.

He made his way down to the river. The water ran wide here. Just a bit upstream, the water rippled over a collection of rocks. At his feet, the river ran fast and clear and he could see the rocky bottom. It would be a lot easier to stand in the river and wash his boots, than to bend over and do it, plus after choking on blast dust, the water looked very inviting. He kicked off his boots, tied them together, and slung them over his shoulder.

He waded in up to his knees. It only took two steps. The cool water felt refreshing.

The steepness of the bottom surprised him, as did the water's depth. But he remembered visiting Lake Tahoe once where the bottom seemed inches away and was really fifty feet deep. This water was at least as clear as Tahoe's.

With the shoes dipped in the water, he scraped the sole of one shoe against the top of the other until he'd scrubbed all the blood from them. Satisfied that he'd rid himself of those morbid reminders, he made a cup with his hands and splashed his face. The invigorating water rinsed the layer of dirt from his skin.

Something splashed upstream. He turned in that direction. The water running down his face blurred his vision. He wiped his eyes clear, but saw nothing. The pattern of ripples in the river seemed different. Maybe the rushing water had dislodged some of the rocks.

Brendan took a deep breath and dunked his head under. He scrubbed his hair with his fingertips and then massaged some dirt from the back of his neck. The sound of stones tumbling on stones rumbled through the water.

He resurfaced and exhaled like a breaching whale. Brendan wiped his face clean and looked all around the river. He was still alone. But this time he was certain that some of the rocks had moved. A string of them about thirty feet long now poked above the water twenty yards upstream.

The water seemed too deep for a pile of rocks to break the surface there. A bad feeling began to percolate deep in his gut. The hairs on the back of his neck went erect.

Suddenly, he was afraid to make a sound. He began a slow, backward creep for shore.

Eyelids popped open within the two closest lumps in the stream. A pair of yellow eyes with red, slit pupils glowered at him.

Brendan's heart slammed into overdrive. Panic swept away caution and he commenced a flailing, splashing retreat from whatever-the-hell was staring at him.

He was still calf-deep in the water when the creature surfaced. It was the largest crocodile he'd ever seen, at least thirty feet long. Its enormous, wide head took up ten of those thirty feet. Its mouth opened and revealed what looked like hundreds of sharp, jagged teeth. The jaws were big enough to swallow him whole.

Brendan splashed ashore and started a barefoot sprint back to the cliff side camp. He'd only taken one step when what felt like a steel clamp closed around both his knees. Bones crunched and he toppled over on his right side. He looked down. The lower half of his leg was somewhere inside the crocodile's snout. Blood spurted from between the creature's teeth. The malevolent yellow eye closest to Brendan glared at him and the pupil narrowed.

Terror had kept Brendan from screaming, but there was no containing his reaction now. He cried out but all his vocal cords could muster was a squeak.

Then with unbelievable speed, the crocodile retreated backward into the stream, dragging Brendan with it. Brendan scraped across the shore and before he could take a breath, he was underwater.

All the motion had churned the river murky. What was up or down all seemed the same. Loss of blood sent Brendan's head reeling. His mouth opened and water poured into his lungs. His body went numb, the world around him went dark. His last thought was wishing he'd never washed his damn boots.

CHAPTER FOURTEEN

Downstream, Priya and Grant stood looking at the footprint near the riverbank.

"Why do you look so white?" Priya said.

"That's no random impression you found," Grant said. "That's a footprint. I've seen enough fossilized examples to know one when I see it."

Priya ran the toe of her shoe across the footprint and smeared the mud. "This one definitely isn't fossilized. What made it?"

"It looks crocodilian to me by the structure, but with some more archaic traits as well."

"How big would the thing that made that footprint be?"

"Well..." Grant didn't like the answer that was about to come out of his mouth. "This print is twice the size of a croc print, so, maybe thirty feet long."

"Please. If there was a thirty-foot-long anything around here, wouldn't we have seen it?"

"You have a point there. The vegetation isn't thick enough to hide an animal that large. The only place that could would be..."

Grant looked out across the river. Just off from where they stood, a pair of twin bumps broke the surface. Each one had a slit-pupiled eye trained on Grant and Priya.

"We need to slowly get away from the water," he said.

"If this is a joke, it isn't funny."

"Most of my jokes aren't, but this isn't one of them. The creature that left that footprint is just under the river's surface."

Priya looked out at the water. Her eyes went wide as she caught sight of the eyes staring back at her. "Oh my God!"

"We'll back away now," Grant said. "No sudden movements."

The two began taking cautious steps away from the river's edge. Then the creature's massive, crocodilian head broke the surface. Water drained off its broad snout. Its mouth opened and revealed more sharp teeth than Grant wanted to count.

"Change of plan," Grant said. "Sudden movements mandatory. Run!"

They both bolted for the cliff. An enormous splash of water sounded behind them. Grant knew that it being from the croc paddling away would be too good to be true. A glance over his shoulder confirmed his fears. The creature was already half out of the water.

He turned to warn Priya, only to find that she was already yards ahead of him. The woman's sprinting skill had just made paleontologist this monster's go-to meal.

He pumped his legs harder and ran pell-mell through the shrubs and trees. Sweat poured from his forehead and every hammer strike of his heart felt like it was about to sever an artery.

From behind him came a deep bellow that made his skin crawl. Bushes snapped followed by the slap of huge reptilian feet against mud and sand. Grant passed into the lee of the canyon overhang and prayed that the creature hunting him would somehow be terrified by this enormous shadow.

A quick look confirmed that the croc was not. The animal was still in hot pursuit and had cut the distance between them in half. And Grant was running out of space.

He rushed uphill. Branches and leaves whipped at him and sliced open his arms. He ducked just in time to miss a branch that would have knocked him flat on his back. Up ahead loomed the canyon wall. Priya leaned against it, panting. A few fallen boulders lay on either side of her. Grant knew they'd offer no protection.

It wasn't in a crocodile's nature to continue the hunt this far from water. Seemed this one hadn't read its own owner's manual.

Why did I have to be so delectable? Grant thought.

Priya had at first looked glad to see Grant coming, then terrified to see the creature right behind him. She looked about for a hiding place. Grant knew there were none.

When he was a dozen yards from Priya, a charley horse turned his left leg muscle to stone. Grant yelped from the pain and pivoted around his locked-up leg.

The creature was headed straight for him. The scientist part of him identified it as a phytosaur. The emotional part of him screamed "Who the hell cares?"

A second from now, his intellectual curiosity about the biting strength of this species would be satisfied, but he'd have been happier using any other method in the world to do it. He closed his eyes.

Upstream, another boom sounded as Terri's crew set off another charge. The ground shook under Grant's feet. Overhead, stone cracked, and a chunk of the overhang above broke free. Grant looked up and the hurtling six-foot-long block of stone looked like it had his name on it.

Beats being eaten, he thought.

The plummeting boulder whizzed by so close in front of his face that he felt the rush of air. It missed Grant but struck the charging phytosaur across the bridge of its open snout. The impact snapped the creature's jaws closed with a crack and drove the animal's head into the sand. It stopped just feet from where Grant stood frozen.

The phytosaur made a whimpering sound, rolled its head sideways, and sent the stone tumbling across the ground. Its jaws met crooked and the rock's impact had shattered multiple teeth. The creature's defeat seemed to have killed its appetite, both for a meal and for further adventures. The phytosaur turned around and headed back to the river. As it did, its long tail whipped around and swept Grant off his feet. He landed butt-first in the sand. The phytosaur disappeared.

Priya ran over to where Grant sat. "Are you okay?"

"I'll need to give my tailbone a close inspection, but other than that I think I survived pretty well."

"You stopped. You were going to sacrifice yourself to save me."

His charley horse had done all the work for him there. Grant hadn't had the presence of mind to think of being so altruistic. But if he had, he certainly would have done what Priya thought he had. Or so he convinced himself.

"Well, one of us had to become a meal. I did have the most meat on my bones."

She hit him on the shoulder. "Good thing for you that falling boulder saved you from such a bad decision."

"I'm definitely taking it home as a souvenir, maybe use it as a paperweight."

Priya helped him to his feet. He gave his left leg a few flexes.

"Of course, now you work," he said under his breath.

"I've seen crocodiles," Priya said. "That was no crocodile."

"No, that was a phytosaur, technically not even a member of the crocodile family."

"It's huge! How could I have never heard of these animals?"

Grant dusted some dirt from his pants. "Because the last one was supposed to have died out 200 million years ago."

"Supposed to?"

"Yes, I'll be updating the Wikipedia page when we get back. It seems that in this little bubble world inside the canyon, the species survived. Just like the archaic hyacinth that impressed zero people other than myself."

"I can't believe that a species surviving that long is possible, but it obviously is."

"As long as the environment is stable or only changes slowly, and there is a food source, a species can continue to thrive."

"I don't want to be a food source," Priya said.

"Neither do I. I have greater ambitions in life. We'll be safer with the large group. We should make our way back."

"Sticking closer to the cliff than the river this time?"

"Oh, absolutely."

CHAPTER FIFTEEN

Terri grumbled a curse and kicked a softball-sized rock up and into the trees around the camp. The last set of charges she had set off had made things worse.

Normally, the way she'd placed and sized the charges would have exposed a new layer of the cliff. Instead, it had brought a much larger section raining down on what was left of the camp. That explosion at the base camp must have weakened the ground a lot more than she'd planned on. The wider swath of exposed surface actually would have been a good thing if some of the crew hadn't been beneath the avalanche when it started.

Terri ruffled her hair to get some of the dirt out of it. Kraus approached her from the other side of the camp. He looked grim.

"It doesn't look like that rock slide damaged any more critical equipment," he said. "But now I can't find Brendan and Carson. The crew thinks they were both near the cliff when it collapsed. It must have buried them."

"How many men does that leave us, then?"

"Eight. Not many."

"But enough to keep going. And if they get weepy over their lost comrades, remind them that the bonus is now split fewer ways."

"Some have already mentioned that."

"See why I like working with mercenaries? Now follow me." Terri scrambled up the debris pile with Kraus following close behind. She paused near the top and pointed to a layer of pink sediment speckled with red. "Get them digging samples from this stratum, every hundred yards or so. The uranium vein will be in there. I'll analyze the samples myself. Whichever one looks most promising, that's where we'll dig deeper."

"You've got it."

Terri noticed Casey a dozen yards away, leaning on a tree and watching her men prepare to get to work. "Casey seems unnaturally interested in our work."

"He's a geology professor," Kraus said, "what would you expect?"

"I'd expect him to be panicked about being isolated in the wilderness like that idiot Coleman is," Terri said. "But he isn't."

"He knows geology, maybe he can help us."

"Not worth the risk. I know what I'm doing. Keep an eye on him. He may get too nosy for his own good."

"And then?"

"This place is dangerous. Accidents happen."

Kraus nodded. "It would have to be accidental. These men are mining mercenaries, but they aren't murderers. Killing college professors might not sit well with all of them."

"Clumsy academics," Terri said, "are the kind who have plenty of mishaps."

***

When Grant and Priya returned to where the Neoborax crew was working, Grant led Priya straight to Terri, who was standing beside a crate and sheafing through papers filled with graphs and tables of numbers. Casey stood beside her.

"Terri, you need to stop everything this group is doing," Grant said, "and start building a place we can defend."

Terri barely glanced in Grant's direction. "To defend against what?"

"There are phytosaurs in the valley."

"Which are what?" Terri said.

"Phytosaurs are crocodile-like creatures, but grow at least twice as large."

Terri's eyes did not look up from the papers on the table. "Is Bigfoot roaming the trees as well?"

"Bigfoot is a myth. Phytosaurs are actual dinosaurs, extinct for 200 million years. Or so I thought."

Terri scoffed. "But now they're alive again?"

"Or always have been. I don't know which, and it doesn't matter. What matters is they are carnivorous and I don't want to be on their menu."

"You saw one of these...phytosaurs?" Casey said.

"From far too close. It chased the two of us from the river to the cliff face."

"It would have killed me," Priya said, "if Grant hadn't offered himself up instead."

Terri looked incredulous and hooked a thumb at Grant. "This guy here tried to stop a charging dinosaur?"

"You think that's hard to believe?" Grant said feigning wounded pride.

"I'm your friend," Casey said, "and *I* think it's hard to believe."

"And you fought this thing off?" Terri said.

"No, a boulder from the cliff fell on it."

"So you can show me the corpse?"

"No, the boulder strike hurt it and scared it off."

Terri leaned forward on the crate and sighed. "So the two of you come running, spouting off a story of a dinosaur run wild, where somehow both of you survived, and conveniently there isn't any physical proof?"

"You'd be happier if it had bitten my arms off?" Grant said.

"I'd certainly be more convinced."

"If that's what Grant and Priya say happened," Casey said, "then I believe them."

"If I wanted a third useless bit of input," Terri said, "I'd ask you for it, Professor. My crew here would have seen something that big if it was here in this canyon."

"Why would I make a story like this up?" Grant said.

"It sounds like a desperate, and I mean *desperate*, attempt to scare us into stopping work. No dice, Coleman. Now I've been willing to leave the three of you alone as long as you stay the hell out of our way." She pointed at Casey. "You've already been borderline annoying watching us work. But the two of you have crossed the line into interfering. Any more crap like this from any of you and I'll bind and gag the lot of you for the duration. Am I clear?"

Grant knew that nothing short of being eaten herself by a phytosaur would convince Terri they existed. She might even deny it as she was being chewed.

Grant threw up his hands. "We tried to warn you. Enjoy being phytosaur treats."

Grant, Priya, and Casey left Terri to her study of the pages on the table. They moved to a spot halfway between the worksite and the river. The location had a view of both spots, but seemed a safe distance from the dangers in each.

"So shoot straight with me," Casey said. "That story was on the level?"

"One hundred percent," Priya said. "We were attacked by a dinosaur."

"And one universal truth about animals," Grant said, "is there's never only one."

"Why wouldn't the Neoborax people have seen one, then?"

"Maybe they stayed closer to the cliff than the river. Maybe some of this blasting they've been doing upset the phytosaur's natural food source and now they want to try a human. All I know is that they're here and they're not in the mood to be patted."

"You study creatures like this," Casey said. "What's our best defense?"

"Don't be the slowest runner," Priya said.

Grant tried to not take that personally. "If the creature has as many crocodilian traits as it seems to, it's going to have a very thick skin, skin tough as hell and hard to penetrate. It lives submerged in water for long periods of time, so it will be impossible to suffocate."

"Other than old age," Priya said, "these things had to die from something."

"Bigger dinosaurs," Grant said. "But that isn't on my list of recommendations."

***

Terri crumpled one of the papers in her hand and banged a fist on the crate. That story from the professors was too stupid to be true. But it was also too stupid to be made up. Grant Coleman was a smartass idiot, but he was intelligent enough to come up with a better story than rampaging phytosaurs. She called over Kraus.

"What kind of wildlife have any of the crew seen around the canyon?" she asked.

"Nothing anyone's mentioned to me. I've seen chipmunk-looking things. Some birds. That kind of stuff."

Of course no one's seen a dinosaur, she thought. *He would have run screaming as soon as he had.*

"Follow me," she said.

Terri led Kraus over to a long crate away from the primary worksite. She swept it clean of dirt and stones from the last avalanche and then grabbed the lock that kept it closed. With a few twists of the dial, the lock popped open. She removed it and threw up the lid.

Inside rested four M-4 military assault rifles in a neat row on a built-in rack. She handed one to Kraus and slung a second one over her shoulder. A stack of loaded magazines rested in the bottom of the crate. She removed two, and gave one of those to Kraus as well.

Kraus gave her a wary look. "What's this for?"

"Any emergency. Animal or human. We need to be prepared."

Kraus shrugged and rammed home the magazine. With a backward sweep of the charging handle, he chambered a round. "You're the boss."

"Nothing's going to slow us down. Nothing."

CHAPTER SIXTEEN

The three professors stood in the shade of a tree to get out of the unrelenting sun.

"I confess," Casey said. "I'm at a loss for what we do now."

"I vote for staying out of Terri's way," Priya said.

"And the phytosaurs' way," Grant said.

His stomach rumbled so loudly that both Priya and Casey looked at him in surprise.

Grant felt his face redden. "Sorry, but it's been a while since breakfast."

"With all that's happened," Priya said, "you can think about food?"

"My stomach is fearless in the face of death."

Priya shook her head and turned to Casey. "Do you think this place is really viable for uranium mining?"

"Assuming it didn't have dinosaurs roaming it," Grant said.

"From what I've observed so far," Casey said, "absolutely. They already uncovered a good-sized roll-front uranium deposit."

"Pretend I'm not one of the most geologically savvy men on earth," Grant said, "and explain what that means."

"Sandstones like those in the canyon are good hosts for roll-front uranium deposits. They look like dull, silver veins in the rock, usually in an easy-to-find line through the stratum. Some of these deposits are enormous. But what really makes them valuable is they can be extracted by in-situ leach recovery."

"That process doesn't sound environmentally friendly," Priya said.

"In that procedure, you drill holes in the ore, frack pathways through it and then pump leaching solution into the deposit. The solution dissolves the uranium, then is pumped to the surface and processed. You can skip expensive conventional mining with all the drilling, blasting, and ore hauling."

"And this location already has plenty of water to do the leaching," Grant said.

"Unlike other nearby locations that may have similar veins of uranium."

"But wouldn't that destroy this valley ecosystem?" Priya said.

"Absolutely. But it's so far away from the rest of the world, by the time someone noticed, it would be gone."

As if on cue, a blast sounded from the canyon wall. The ground vibrated hard enough that Grant steadied himself against the tree. He turned to see a dusty cloud rising from near the worksite.

"Terri and this crew don't seem at all worried about safety, the environment, or the workers who've died," Priya said.

"And she just added dinosaurs to that list," Grant said.

A huge splash in the river drew Grant's attention from the cliff. But all he saw was a stripe of white water that the current quickly erased.

Grant exhaled. "Good. For a minute I was afraid I was going to see—"

Two enormous phytosaur snouts rose from the river at the water's edge.

"—something like that," he finished.

The three of them sprinted uphill to the worksite. Grant didn't waste any effort in turning around to see if they were being pursued. He was willing to assume they were.

Sounds at the river confirmed his assumption. A violent splashing of water was followed by the slap of huge feet on wet sand and then the crunch of branches.

Casey glanced over his shoulder. The color drained from his face. "Oh, hell. They're coming! Grant, how fast can they run?"

"Too fast."

Priya and Casey accelerated. Grant was already in top gear and his leg muscles were ready to call it a day. He fell behind.

Priya and Casey entered the worksite area. The whole crew seemed to be up near the base of the cliff, inspecting the results of the last charge.

"Run!" Casey shouted. "Everyone!"

The aftereffects of the blast seemed to have dulled their hearing, because few of them reacted to Casey's warning. The ones who did just gave Casey an annoyed look.

Grant lumbered up to where Terri was turning a football-sized chunk of rock over in one hand. She still had earmuff hearing protection on. Grant noted the rifle now slung over one shoulder as an unwelcome accessory. She noticed him and pulled her hearing protection off with her free hand.

If more running was required to stay alive, Grant resigned himself to a horrific death. He stopped and, wheezing, rested his hands on both knees.

"What now?" Terri said.

"Those dinosaurs you say can't still be alive?" Grant pointed a thumb in the direction of the river. "Here some come."

Terri turned as the two phytosaurs came crashing through the brush. She whipped the rifle off her shoulder. "Kraus!"

A number of the crew saw the dinosaurs and sent up cries of alarm. Kraus came running from the edge of the worksite with a rifle at the ready. He stood by Terri and both of them took aim at the creatures. The phytosaurs were thirty yards away.

Grant didn't know much about firearms, but he knew about dinosaur and crocodile skin. He didn't think any bullets were going to make much difference. He stood up and raised a hand to start his warning.

He was too late. Both Neoborax employees fired. At this range, it didn't seem likely they could miss. But if the shots hit the creatures, Grant couldn't tell. The phytosaurs kept coming.

Grant didn't have one more stride's worth of energy in him. He dropped down behind a crate and hoped for a miracle.

It came. The phytosaurs charged past him, headed for Terri and Kraus. The two emptied several more rounds into the dinosaurs and then sprinted a retreat when the animals didn't stop. They made their way through the maze of tents and materials between their position and the dynamited cliff face. The rest of the crew were dashing off in all directions.

The phytosaurs charged headlong into the worksite. Crates and equipment went flying as the animals smashed their way through. One of the phytosaurs roared and charged a tent with a flapping door that must have seemed like foundering prey. It barreled through the canvas side and collapsed the tentpoles at the corners. The canvas dropped on the dinosaur and it roared against being blinded.

It spun around and tried to shake the tent off. But each revolution further tangled the ropes around the creature's front legs and bound the canvas trap tighter around the animal's head. The phytosaur began a rolling, thrashing attempt to tear off the heavy canvas.

The other phytosaur wasn't deterred by its companion's dilemma. It charged through the camp for the human prey at the cliff's edge. Terri, Kraus, and several men had climbed up eight feet to a ledge carved out by a previous round of blasting. They held shovels and picks that had been left on the ledge, but Grant knew if that was their only dinosaur defense, they might as well have had none at all.

Another man had beaten them there and was free-climbing the cliff a few yards above the ledge. The phytosaur got to the base of the cliff, opened its mouth and bellowed.

The climber shuddered at the sound, and then lost his grip. He screamed, fell backward and missed the ledge. He landed back-first on the ground with a thud, just a few feet from the phytosaur. The man looked up at the creature and shrieked.

The phytosaur did not refuse this offering. With a sideways snap of its jaws, it clamped the hapless worker and a collection of small branches in its teeth. It swallowed the man whole. A struggling human form stretched the skin as it slid down the phytosaur's neck. Then the phytosaur growled and, with the hunt complete, returned to the river.

With the second phytosaur still flailing around at the edge of the camp, Grant took this opportunity to make for what looked like safer ground, the outcropping the Neoborax people had claimed. He stumbled through the camp's wreckage to the rocks that made up the makeshift steps to the ledge. In the last five minutes he'd done more exercise than in the last six months. At the base of the rocks, his pounding heart and throbbing feet cried out "enough." He crawled up the pile on his hands and knees.

Grant heaved himself onto the ledge and rolled onto his back, panting hard.

"Seriously," he said to himself. "I have to get back in shape when I get home. Gym membership, first thing."

Terri stepped over and looked down at him with contempt. "I was sure those things had killed you."

"Not dead yet."

The sound of tearing canvas came from the camp's edge. Grant rose to his knees and looked over the edge. The second phytosaur rolled onto its feet with a collar of shredded canvas around its neck. It searched the area, as if looking for someone to exact revenge upon for this indignation. It paused at the base of the cliff. Everyone on the ledge froze in place.

The idea that he was about to observe whether a phytosaur hunted by scent, sight, or sound would have been much more welcome to Grant had he not been the object of the hunt.

One of the Neoborax people spoiled the experiment. He took a step and inadvertently sent a cascade of dirt and rocks down from the ledge. One bounced off the phytosaur's snout. The phytosaur whipped its head up and around and locked its eyes on the people on the ledge. The red, slit pupils gave Grant chills.

The phytosaur lunged for the cliff. The narrow ledge was only eight feet off the ground. While this seemed an insurmountable height when Grant was climbing it, he feared it would be no impediment at all for a thirty-foot crocodile. The dinosaur crashed into the earth beneath them. The ledge shook. Grant jumped to his feet and slammed his back against the cliff wall.

The dinosaur roared and started to climb. Just like a crocodile, the phytosaur was an ungainly climber, limited by the short, squat legs that protruded from its sides. Grant harbored the faint hope that perhaps all of them were safe on the ledge.

But the phytosaur adapted. It dug in its claws and used its thick tail to push itself higher. Its front feet scrambled against the cliff face and claws tore at the dirt. The phytosaur made a little progress and its snout came closer to the ledge.

Once again Grant dared hope that he was out of the creature's reach.

Then he noticed the phytosaur's impact on the cliff. As it scoured away the dirt, the ledge's edge began to crumble. Even if it never made it any higher, the dinosaur would soon weaken the ledge to the point where all of them tumbled down to become a buffet meal.

Kraus grabbed a rag from the ground and a five gallon can. He moved to the edge of the ledge, just above the creature's snout. He tossed away the top of the can and dropped it down on its side. A strong, sharp chemical scent filled the air. A clear liquid gushed out across the ground, over the edge, and onto the phytosaur's snout. The creature paused and shook its head as the liquid ran down onto the canvas that encircled its neck.

More of the ledge broke up and rolled downhill. The snout rose again.

Kraus pulled a lighter from his pocket and lit the rag afire. He dropped it on the spilled liquid.

The liquid trail turned into a ribbon of orange flame. Globs of fire dripped from the ledge and set the phytosaur's snout ablaze. Flames raced down its jaws all the way to the canvas around the phytosaur's neck. The soaked cloth burst into flame.

The phytosaur emitted a squealing scream as it twisted its head back and forth. It lost its grip on the ground and tumbled backward from the cliff. With a crash it landed on its side and then rolled over onto its feet. It thrashed in vain to shake the burning ring from its neck. An awful smell like charred, rancid meat filled the air. The phytosaur bellowed and bolted in the direction of the river, vanishing into the woods.

Grant slumped down onto what remained of the ledge. The other Neoborax men exhaled in relief. Kraus kicked the empty five-gallon can off the ledge. The miners came over and congratulated him.

Terri looked out across the canyon, pointedly not at Grant.

"You were right," Grant said. "Imagine me trying to get you to believe dinosaurs roamed this canyon."

CHAPTER SEVENTEEN

The survivors of the attack climbed down from the crumbling ledge. Grant's descent was more of a controlled slide and bounce.

"What was that you ignited?" Casey asked Kraus.

"Acetone," Kraus said. "We use it to clean contaminated metal in a flash."

"And it doubles as a good dinosaur repellent," Casey said.

Terri shouted for all the Neoborax employees to gather. A few joined the group from nearby in the woods. When they'd assembled, there were seven including Kraus. The largest of the men wore a hard hat with CRUSHER written on the front with a fat magic marker. Where the rest of the workers looked scared, Crusher looked mad enough to grab a chunk of sandstone and live up to his name.

"Someone want to explain what the hell just happened here?" Crusher said. "Ain't none of us signed up to be in no Godzilla movie."

"Neither did I," Terri said. "This guy here has all the answers."

Terri directed their attention to Grant. Every head swiveled in his direction. Crusher's eyes narrowed and he balled his fists. Grant swallowed hard. Not only did he not have all the answers, he wasn't even done coming up with all the questions.

"Well," Grant said as he pushed his glasses up the bridge of his nose, "those were phytosaurs and it seems like they've been living in this valley long after they went extinct everywhere else in the world."

"How long?" one worker asked.

"A couple of hundred million years. A tick of the clock in geologic time."

Grant offered a weak smile at his joke. No one joined him.

"What pissed them off?" Crusher said.

"Seems that the two of them that attacked were in search of a meal."

"The two of them?" Kraus said. "You mean there's more than two out there?"

"I'd have to say yes to that."

"Getting out of here just became a priority over finding the uranium," Kraus said to Terri.

Grant waited for Terri to object. She didn't.

"There's still no way out except by rescue," she said. "So we need to find a safe place to hole up."

"The village in the sky," Priya said.

Everyone's attention turned to Priya. Grant was thrilled to be out of the hot seat.

"What are you talking about?" Terri said.

"There are ancient cliffside dwellings a mile or two downriver," Priya said. "They are too high up for the phytosaurs to climb."

"But that's miles of walking," Crusher said. "Miles where we attract more giant crocodiles. No way in hell."

"Plus," Kraus added, "some of the guys are hurt."

"We'll stay here," Terri said. "This is where a rescue team will be looking for us. We'll have to find a way to defend ourselves."

Kraus held up his rifle. "And these aren't any help."

"We have the explosives you've been mining with," Grant said. "Let's throw them at the phytosaurs."

"They aren't nitroglycerin," Kraus said. "They're harmless unless they're properly triggered."

"Then we'll make them into bombs and throw them."

Kraus rolled his eyes. "It isn't like in action movies where someone straps a timer to one. You have to set a blasting cap in the explosives, then trigger the cap with an electrical charge."

"Next," Grant said, "you'll be telling me we can't set one off by shooting it with a bullet."

"I'll pretend you aren't dumb enough to think that."

"Of course not," Grant said. "Who'd be that stupid?"

"We can't throw the charges at the dinosaurs," Terri said, "but we *can* get the dinosaurs to come to the charges. Kraus, have the charges set in a semi-circle around the ledge, close enough that we can see them but far enough away that when they blow we won't become casualties."

"You want an anti-dinosaur minefield?" Kraus said.

"Exactly. We'll wait it out behind that line until Neoborax people stick their heads over the canyon rim and get us out of here. Every dino goes boom." She turned to Grant. "Tell me one of the charges we have will kill one of those damned things."

"If it will blast solid rock, it will shred the toughest reptile skin."

"Since we kicked their asses," Crusher said, "they should know better than to come messing with us again."

"That could be," Grant said. "One isn't hungry anymore. The other is off metaphorically licking its wounds. Animals generally shy away from situations where they've been hurt in the past."

"Perfect." Terri motioned to two men near the cliff base. "You two shore up and expand the ledge. The rest of you come with me. We'll set the remains of the camp up to block part of the way to the ledge and channel the dinosaurs to where we have the charges set. When it's done, I'll set the schedule for who's on guard with their fingers on the triggers."

"What do you want us to do?" Casey said.

"Not much any of you are qualified to do. Why don't you keep a watch from the ledge so we don't get ambushed by those things?"

Grant compared that menial task with risking blowing himself up or manhandling debris into barricades and he liked Terri's idea much more. He followed Priya and Casey up onto the ledge. The three of them took seats against the cliff looking out across the worksite.

"The good news is," Grant said, "we found out there's something worse than just being unwilling members of an illegal mining operation."

"This situation has gone from bad to worse," Casey said. "I'm even sorrier that I brought you two out here."

"I did discover a new Native American tribe," Priya said. "If I live to tell anyone about it."

"Once they set those charges around the camp," Casey said, "I'm sure we'll be okay. We're two hundred million years of evolution ahead of the phytosaurs. Right, Grant?"

"Absolutely," Grant said.

But what he was thinking was that phytosaurs were millions of evolutionary years ahead of humans in becoming hunters while humans had nearly forgotten how to not become prey.

Over the next few hours, Grant watched as the Neoborax workers set charges in the open areas approaching the worksite. They buried the blocks of explosives a foot or so underground, with scrap metal wreckage just on top of the charge. Each detonation would not only have an explosive impact, but it would also act like a giant, wide-range shotgun. Grant was very glad he wasn't a phytosaur. Then the men unspooled a set of wires from each charge and walked them back to a spot by the cliff. Grant couldn't see that area too clearly, but there was a chair, a table, a row of switches and what looked like a large battery wired in under the table. As soon as the first charge was connected to a switch, one of the Neoborax men took a seat behind it.

The knowledge that someone was ready to defend them set Grant a bit more at ease. His stomach growled.

Priya gave him a disapproving look. "Again?"

Grant's face reddened. "Sorry. I guess living in abject terror makes me hungry."

"There's still some packs of trail mix and protein bars by that table over there," Casey said.

"When you're dying for a cheeseburger, trail mix is a pretty poor substitute."

"You'd be surprised what a vegan diet can do to your outlook on the day," Priya said.

"I know exactly what it would do," Grant said. "It would ruin it."

Casey hadn't taken his eyes off the people setting up the protective perimeter. "The Neoborax people are putting together a solid defensive semi-circle out there. It should be more of an obstacle than a dinosaur would expect. They'll walk through the gaps and then boom."

Grant thought his friend might be right. In most instances, despite their great size, dinosaurs generally had brains the size of a small fruit. They wouldn't have the mental capacity to understand they were being funneled into a kill zone.

At least he hoped that was true.

CHAPTER EIGHTEEN

Since the ledge was less than spacious, Terri announced that the survivors would spend the night sleeping on the ground around a fire set up well inside the half-moon of explosives. Even Crusher the Malcontented had no objections to that plan.

Terri set up shifts among the Neoborax men to man the detonators as well as keep a watch on the perimeter. As the canyon's early dusk fell, the first two in the rotation took their positions. Dinner ended up being a ration of the dried foods that had been intended as snacks. The small portions Kraus distributed to each person told Grant that he and Terri were thinking rescue wasn't right around the corner.

Grant, Priya, and Casey sat together on one side of the fire. Grant looked with dismay at the remaining half of the protein bar he'd eaten. It was hard to believe that a company could make something coated in chocolate taste lousy, but this one sure had.

"We didn't rate a role in the night's defensive watch," Casey said.

"I can assure everyone," Grant said, "that the last thing this group needs is me manning the switches on bundles of explosives."

"We could at least have taken our share of watching the perimeter," Casey said.

"Terri has wisely decided that our keen intellects need a good night's rest to face the rigors of tomorrow," Grant said.

"Or she doesn't trust us," Priya said.

"It could also be that. Whatever the reason, I will not let the opportunity for a night of sleep pass me by."

"You'll be able to sleep with those giant lizards roaming around?" Priya said.

Grant stopped himself from correcting her "lizard" appellation. "I'm guessing that the phytosaurs are diurnal. Their eyes don't seem adapted to night vision and similar creatures are daylight hunters. Cold blooded creatures also have a hard time regulating body heat, and usually rest in the cooler evening."

"So you feel safe?" Casey said.

"Sure, as long as some other supposedly extinct creature hasn't filled the night shift niche."

"Way to go Mr. Half Empty Glass," Casey said. "If they are up at night, the fire will keep the phytosaurs away."

"Assuming the animals here naturally fear fire," Grant said. "It could be they've never experienced it in this narrow, isolated canyon. The phytosaur that got the flaming canvas necklace treatment sure has, but it's not like he has the vocal skills to tell any others his story."

"You have a knack for building a thundercloud in a clear blue sky," Casey said.

"It's more a gift," Grant said.

Despite his voiced and unvoiced concerns about their overnight safety, Grant hoped he'd be able to get a good night's sleep. He'd slept like crap on the way here and this full day of danger and unwelcome exercise had been exhausting.

Darkness fell, he lay down, and the wretchedness of his situation became apparent. He'd found the most level-looking ground he could, and still it seemed like there were a dozen rocks beneath him doing their best impression of a bed of nails. His arm took the place of a pillow until the uncomfortable angle made his shoulder ache. Then every time he nodded off, he jolted awake to some innocuous sound outside the firelight that his imagination had amplified into impending doom. Despite longing for a night's rest, misery drove him to crave the dawn.

As soon as there was enough light to see beyond the campfire, Grant was up stretching his cramped muscles. He shook out his arms and legs, then caught his own scent, which was a noxious combination of sweat and burning wood. If a dip in the river hadn't meant he'd become a phytosaur breakfast, he would have welcomed it.

What smelled much better was coffee someone had brewed over the fire. The pot sat on a table on the other side of the fire beside large containers of sugar and creamer. Grant wished there were bacon and eggs to go with it, but he'd take what he could get. He wondered how he could hunt up a cup.

Priya rolled over and looked up at Grant in disbelief. "You are awake already? Were you up all night on watch?"

"As far as you know, yes. And as a result, we're all safe and sound."

Casey came walking up from the edge of the worksite. His shirt was wet.

"How did you get wet?" Grant said.

"A quick wash in the river," Casey said. "My aroma demanded it. And you aren't far behind in that category."

"Better to stink and not be dinosaur food."

"I went because you said the phytosaurs wouldn't be up and about until it was daylight."

"I said that was my theory," Grant said. "I didn't expect you to bet your life on it."

"I'll go back to my usual plan of dismissing everything you say, then." Casey handed Grant and Priya some protein bars. "Breakfast is served. No one blew anything up last night, so that's good."

From the far side of the camp Kraus shouted for Terri. Grant didn't like the panic in his voice. Grant and the other two moved in Kraus' direction. Terri rose from where she was sleeping and sprinted there ahead of them.

Grant arrived to see Kraus standing beside one of the spots where they'd placed an explosive charge. Two wires stuck out of a hole in the ground and the metal bits that were destined to become shrapnel lay scattered all around. The explosive was gone.

"What the hell happened?" Terri said.

"I don't know," Kraus said. "Robinson had the watch. I couldn't find him. So I started looking to see if he'd fallen asleep somewhere. I didn't find him, but I did find this hole. The explosives are gone."

Casey walked a few feet into the woods. "And you'd better see this."

The four of them gathered around. A puddle of dried blood sat on the ground. More blood speckled the leaves.

Crusher came running over to the group. He looked at the hole in the ground with dismay.

"Terri, all the other charges we set yesterday? They're just like that one. Dug up and gone."

"Damn it," Terri said.

"One of those dinosaurs got Robinson," Casey said. "And then dug up our entire line of defense."

"I thought these things had brains the size of lemons," Priya said to Grant.

"They do," Grant said. "Or they should. But if they can do this, those brains are much more developed than anyone believed."

"We're sitting ducks out here, now," Kraus said.

Just then, a phytosaur bellowed from off in the woods.

CHAPTER NINETEEN

Everyone at the worksite froze. Grant's pulse went into overdrive. Their only line of defense was gone. Priya's "don't be the slowest runner" recommendation rang in his ears and he had a bad feeling he wasn't going to be able to follow it.

Kraus and Terri went for their rifles. The weapons hadn't beaten back the phytosaurs before, but maybe it gave the two of them a feeling that they were less than helpless. The remaining Neoborax crew retreated to around the burning fire.

From the bushes in the center, a phytosaur's head extended into the clearing. It hissed and then moved further in, exposing the red, raw ring around its neck.

"That's the phytosaur we burned in their last attack," Casey said.

"And it isn't going to let bygones be bygones," Grant said.

Then on either side of the creature, two more phytosaurs came out of the woods.

"Great," Grant said. "He brought friends."

Kraus and Terri took aim and fired. Terri's round sang as it ricocheted off phytosaur hide. But Kraus had taken special aim at the creature's weakest spot, and at this range didn't miss. His bullet struck the left-most phytosaur in the eye. The dinosaur's eye exploded with a splash of blood and liquid.

The phytosaur screamed in a high-pitched wail that made shearing metal sound soothing. The creature shook its head, as if trying to dislodge whatever had just punctured its eye. Failing that it slammed that blinded side of its head against a tree.

The other two seemed ready to revenge the damage done to their brother. They came charging into the camp, legs scrambling and tails sweeping behind them.

Everyone scattered. One Neoborax man had already climbed atop the stone ledges. Grant had the burned dinosaur following hard on his heels. The ledge seemed miles away.

But just ahead of the rampaging phytosaur, Grant made it to the base of the cliff. The man on the ledge turned around and bent down to give Grant a hand up.

The pursuing phytosaur pivoted around its front feet and its body made a clockwise sweep across the camp. Several boxes and camp chairs went flying past Grant, and then the huge tail hit him. It felt like a giant leather tube smacked him on the side. He lost his footing and the dinosaur swept him off his feet.

The creature's tail hit the ground, but Grant kept going. Momentum launched him into the air and back into the campsite. Ahead, the campfire flames licked the air, right in his path. He sailed straight over the fire and felt the flames' heat cross his body. He landed on the other side and rolled into the table holding the morning's coffee. The table flipped onto its side, the pot sailed away spraying a fan of brown liquid, and the coffee condiments hit the ground all around him. The dinosaur looked at him from across the fire and Grant swore it grinned.

Then the phytosaur whipped its tail across the ledge where the Good Samaritan who tried to help Grant still stood in shock. The tail struck the man edge-first and ripped him practically in half. Blood and organs sprayed across the ledge. The corpse fell to the ground and lay in what would have otherwise been an impossible V-shape. The phytosaur whirled around and swallowed half the corpse in one bite.

The other phytosaur crashed through the site, smashing anything it came into contact with. Casey and Priya had a head start uphill, but one of the workers was not as swift. The phytosaur caught up with him, and with a twist of its head brought its jaws down on the man. He screamed in a pitch that made Grant's ears hurt, then went silent with his head sticking out one side of the creature's jaws and his legs the other. The phytosaur made a rumbling noise and settled down to eat.

A quick look around the camp told Grant that everyone had made their way to someplace safer. Everyone but him.

He rationalized that the phytosaurs were here for a meal. He'd seen them retreat after eating. Both of these creatures had a gruesome private feast going on. Neither were looking in his direction. All he had to do was slowly get up, quietly walk away, and these two would stick with finishing breakfast.

I can do this, he thought.

He swore a voice in his head said "No way in hell you can." It sounded annoyingly like his ex-wife.

He opted to ignore the voice. Grant rose to his feet. Smashing into the table had spawned a plethora of aches and pains in parts of his body he didn't know could hurt. He took one careful step toward the trees.

The box of sugar packets crunched under his foot.

The burned dinosaur spun around to face Grant. Half the dead man lay unconsumed on the ground. The dinosaur's eyes narrowed as they locked on Grant from across the campfire. Eating seemed to be a secondary consideration for this one. Grant got the distinct impression the burned phytosaur was out for revenge. It took a half-step closer to him.

Grant wasn't going to outrun it. But he'd go down fighting. Rocks from the blasts salted the ground all around his feet. Keeping his eyes on the phytosaur, he reached down for one. He came up with something much lighter.

He held the gallon container of granulated non-dairy creamer from the coffee table.

"Damn it," he sighed.

Before he could drop it for something more effective, the phytosaur roared. The noise and the stink of its hot breath sent Grant into a panic. In an automatic response, he threw the creamer container at the beast, and immediately realized the futile stupidity of the act.

As the container sailed over the fire, the lid popped off. A cloud of cream-colored particles filled the air.

Then they exploded.

With a white flash and a deep boom, the very air over the fire detonated. The blast blew Grant backward and onto his butt. The light flash-blinded him and the sound sent his ears ringing. His head spun and throwing up became a very real possibility.

The muffled cries of the phytosaurs and the stomp of dinosaur footfalls eked past the ringing in his ears. The bright white that had washed out the world faded and the worksite reappeared. He cleaned the dust from his glasses.

The phytosaurs were gone. The explosion had blown out the fire and scattered its charred, glowing remains in a wide circle around the firepit. Ash caked the front of Grant's shirt. He spat a chunk of wood from between his lips.

"What do you know," he said. "Still not dead."

The coffee pot sat on the ground beside him. Something had pierced it through and through. Grant's first thought was joy that he hadn't gotten the same treatment. Then sadness crept back in as he realized there'd be no coffee for the duration of the canyon stay.

The ringing in his ears dialed down to a background hum. He used the toppled table to help get to his feet. As he did, members of the Neoborax team began a cautious return to the worksite. Casey and Priya went straight for Grant.

"Are you all right?" Casey said.

"Shaken like one of those balls in a spray paint can," Grant said, "but mostly in one piece."

"What was that explosion?"

"Coffee creamer. I threw it and—"

"Quick thinking!" Casey said. "Dispersed as a fine powder, that stuff is explosively flammable."

"I would have never been calm enough to think that through," Priya said.

Grant hadn't remotely been calm enough to think it through. He didn't even know creamer was flammable. He'd never stir it into his coffee again for fear of setting off an explosion in his mug.

"You know me," Grant said, "I thrive in an emergency situation. Mr. Cool they call me."

"I don't think they do," Casey said.

"They do it behind your back so you don't feel threatened."

Kraus went to the severed corpse of the Good Samaritan and gagged as he saw it. He looked across the camp and saw where the other phytosaur had severed the worker's head from his body and left it on the ground during its retreat. He cursed under his breath.

Terri walked over to where the three were standing by the remains of the firepit. She surveyed the worksite. "Well, this is an irretrievable mess now."

"*And* you're officially out of creamer," Grant said.

Terri called that the area was clear and for everyone to come out. Crusher was the only one who came out of the woods.

Kraus stepped up beside Terri. "Two dead at the cliff and Lawton and Triana are also crushed at the edge of camp. Others might have survived, but who knows where they've run off to. I think this is everyone we have left."

"Three professors, two managers and one worker," Terri said. "Not a promising drilling team."

"The drilling equipment's ruined now anyway," Kraus said.

"Can't we set new charges to defend ourselves from the dinosaurs?" Priya said.

"There aren't enough explosives now," Terri said. "And the damn dinosaurs are smart enough to dig them up anyway."

"We could still go to the village in the sky," Grant said. "It would be safe and we have a window of time now where the dinosaurs are disoriented and in retreat."

"How far away is this place?" Terri said.

"A mile or two down the canyon," Priya said.

Terri sighed and stared at her feet. She looked up. "Save anything you can carry. We're going to the village in the sky."

CHAPTER TWENTY

Everyone had their own priorities about what to bring to the village in the sky. Grant's priority was sustenance. He went straight to the cases of food in the storage area.

The phytosaur rampage had not been kind to them. A number were crushed and the bags of trail mix within burst open. The protein bars had fared better. Even a phytosaur couldn't crush the little bricks. No wonder Grant had a hard time chewing them. He stuffed his pockets with the loose ones, picked up the surviving case, and walked over to Priya. She had two one-gallon water containers at her feet.

"Assuming our digestive tracts can do a better job on these bars than our teeth can," Grant said as he shook the box of protein bars, "we won't starve. At least not right away."

"Only one of these water containers is full," she said. "When we think it's safe, we can refill them at the river."

Grant decided he would see how well he could imitate a camel before he got that close to phytosaur-infested water.

Casey stepped up with a roll of maps in one hand. "These may help us find a way out of here if rescue doesn't arrive."

Crusher brought over a big bundle of serviceable tent canvas. Kraus carried a box of ammunition for the rifles. Terri had a backpack across her shoulders.

"I have all the medical supplies that survived the rampage," she said, "plus the samples we dug."

"Splendid," Grant said. "You can throw them at the phytosaurs when they attack."

"They are the only fruits of our labor down here," Terri said, "and I plan on needing them because I plan on us getting out of here alive."

"I left a few notes for the rescue team on the equipment," Kraus said, "telling them where we went. I also warned them about the dinosaurs."

"In my experience," Grant said, "Neoborax people don't take dinosaur warnings seriously."

"Well, they'll see that something wrecked the camp. They can call it whatever they want."

"Let's roll," Terri said. "Priya, lead the way. You know where we're going."

Priya nodded and headed uphill toward the base of the cliff. Grant fell in behind her. Casey ended up in the rear behind the three Neoborax people. Grant's body still hadn't forgiven him for all the abuse he'd subjected it to since waking up, so every step was painful. In addition, it did not take long before what had seemed like the manageable weight of the protein bar case soon made his arms sing a soulful lament.

"Maybe once we get up closer to the canyon rim," Priya said, "we can get a cell signal and call for help."

"Maybe." Grant knew that wouldn't happen. They hadn't had a cell signal at the camp on the rim, and if for some reason one was out there now, it wasn't going to penetrate the solid rock over the village in the sky. But who was he to crush Priya's hopes? He'd let reality do it later.

After a while, they got to where the steps were cut into the canyon wall. The group rested for a few moments.

Terri looked up at the structures overhead. "Damn, those look like they were carved out of the rock itself."

"They probably started that way," Priya said. "I'm sure the native people began with a natural cave or ledge, but they expanded it to this village with adobe over who knows how many centuries."

"Why the hell would someone live up there on the side of a cliff?" Kraus said.

"Maybe because there were dinosaurs running around in the canyon?" Grant said.

Kraus gave Grant an irked look. "No kidding. But why stay here at all? If you can climb this high, you can climb out completely and leave the dinos alone."

"That's a good question," Priya said. "One that was asked about the Anastasi, and one that will be asked about these people as well."

From upstream near the river came the bellow of a phytosaur. Everyone jumped to their feet. Grant rose with a moan.

"Let's climb," Terri said.

"I'll take a turn with that box," Casey said.

Relieved beyond measure, Grant handed him the box. "You're a gentleman and a scholar."

Priya groaned as she lifted the water jugs. Terri placed a hand on her shoulder.

"Take a break with those since you're climbing first," she said. "The Coffee Creamer Hero can take them up."

Grant thought there was no way he could carry them up the steps. He'd be lucky to get himself up there again.

Then he saw the relieved look on Priya's face.

"No problem." Grant adopted a manly, devil-may-care attitude he hoped didn't seem as fake as it was.

Priya began her climb. Grant followed. The weights in each hand seemed to be fighting each other over which got to throw him off balance to plummet into Desolation Canyon. In no time he was sweating and out of breath.

This time Casey was right behind Grant. "How's it going, buddy?"

"Fantastic," Grant said. "But I think the altitude is starting to get to me."

"Pretty sure we're below sea level."

"No wonder I'm drowning in my own sweat."

After what Grant could swear was sixteen hours, they finally made it to the initial lookout post where Grant and Priya had stopped earlier. Grant let the water jugs drop to the floor and he leaned against a wall. The rest of the party followed him up.

Casey, annoyingly un-winded, looked out over the valley floor. "That's a hell of a view."

"And it comes with a warning." Grant pointed to the carving in the floor of the stick man being attacked by a phytosaur.

"Dear God," Casey said.

"Looks like you were right about that carving, Grant," Priya said.

"I wish I hadn't been."

"They could see the whole valley from here," Priya said. "It's the perfect lookout position."

"For what?" Terri said. "A dinosaur wasn't going to scale those steps, and no hostile Indian is going to climb down into that canyon."

Grant agreed that really was a good question. There had to be a damn good reason for a primitive tribe to invest all the effort into creating a suspended city like this, especially doing it by hand.

Priya smiled. "Maybe we'll find out as we explore this place."

Grant was much more up for resting than exploring, but he pushed himself off the wall. "Can't wait."

Priya led them up the next set of steps. Grant got a better look at the village this time. These steps ended at a huge, open plaza. A floor of impossibly perfectly square stones stretched out at least fifty yards. Many contained carved hieroglyphs.

At the far end rose a three-story structure that looked at least partially hewn from the rock behind it. A single door on the first floor offered access. Window openings promised a number of rooms on each floor. Several other structures stood just beyond it. Along the wall on the right ran a building that looked more like an old roadside motel than anything else. Identical door and window pairs ran the entire fifty-yard length. The area was remarkably clean. The overhanging roof seemed to have kept the weather in the canyon and most of the dust from the desert above out.

Terri paused to check if her phone had a signal. Her cursing response told Grant the answer there was no.

"Spread out," Terri said. "See if these people were smart enough to build a stairway to the canyon rim."

Grant and Casey walked to the building at the far end of the plaza. Grant pushed open the wooden door. It hung on what looked like leather hinges. They creaked loudly, then crumbled to bits. The door crashed down onto the floor.

"Guess I don't know my own strength," Grant said.

Grant and Casey entered.

This first-floor room was about 10'x20'. The far wall was the unfinished cliff face, with a set of stairs to the next floor carved into it.

A variety of stone tools leaned against the other three block walls, ranging from crude axes to what looked like hoes. A simple, sturdy table sat in the middle. A partial skull of a phytosaur took up the middle of the table.

Casey went to inspect the tools, but Grant went straight for the skull. He lifted it up for a better inspection. It was no fossil, this was still actual bone, and age hadn't yellowed or weakened it.

"These tools are all made from harder volcanic rock," Casey said as he inspected the head of a spear. "These had to come from the layers closer to the canyon floor."

Grant glanced over at the weapon Casey held. "Priya showed me a hand ax that looked like it was made the same way those were."

"This room isn't right," Casey said. "Even protected from the elements like this place is, if the people living here died off a thousand years ago, this room would have had sand blown into it. And the leather strips binding this arrowhead aren't a thousand years old."

"And the door hinges would have rotted away," Grant said. "Plus, it wasn't that long ago that a little brain was working away inside this phytosaur skull. But if that's true—"

Just then, Priya's scream cut him off mid-sentence.

CHAPTER TWENTY-ONE

Casey and Grant bolted from the room. Across the plaza, Priya stood outside one of the rooms staring into an open door. They ran for her. Terri, Crusher, and Kraus did the same from the other side of the compound.

Grant skidded to a stop beside Priya. "Are you okay?"

"Yes," she said, embarrassed. "The room next to this one was empty. I came here, pushed open the door, and they startled me."

On the floor lay four bodies: a man, a woman, and two children. They lay on mats woven out of the reeds that grew along the riverbanks. Each wore minimal, simple, leather loincloths, the woman also sported a kind of tunic. All had long, black hair, the woman's in a single braid. Their skin had shrunken around their bones, but even taking that into account, the four were undersized and didn't seem like they'd been robust when alive.

The far wall of the room was rough-hewn rock, but the other three walls were finished sandstone blocks, some with crude paintings on them. Along one wall sat a collection of pottery vessels and smaller stone tools.

Kraus knelt down beside the bodies. He nudged one with the barrel of his rifle.

"I've seen a lot of dead bodies," he said.

Grant didn't want the details on how that had happened.

"These haven't been dead that long," Kraus continued. "Definitely not a thousand years."

Priya approached and bent down for a closer examination. "Yes. The dry air has helped with preservation, but these are not mummified remains. These people were living and breathing not that long ago."

"That explains why the workshop we were in looked recently used." Grant peered into an open pottery container in the corner. "And there's water in this container, and I'm going to go out on a limb and say it's not from a recent rain. But the steps up here were covered in dirt when we discovered them, like they hadn't been used."

"All lightweight sand," Priya said. "Probably sent sliding off the cliff face by mining vibrations."

"There don't appear to be any wounds on any of them," Terri said. "They all just died in their sleep together?"

Casey stood beside a fissure in the back wall. It ran along the bottom near the floor and was about half an inch wide. He ran a finger along the inside and then held it up to the light. Green and yellow dust coated his fingertip.

"They didn't just die," Casey said. "They were asphyxiated. This fissure is new, and these are volcanic minerals deposited all along the edge. When this crack opened up, it released trapped gasses from the rock behind and beneath it. Those kinds of gasses can be ripe with carbon monoxide. Enough of them, in a closed space, would make sure none of these people ever woke up."

"And we're just going to stand in here and become a new group of victims?" Crusher said.

"I don't feel anything venting now, and if the atmosphere was still toxic, we'd have all been dead already. No, this stone ripped open recently."

"Triggered by these idiots dynamiting the canyon walls, maybe?" Priya said.

Terri's face flushed red with anger.

"More than likely," Casey said. "But not the dynamiting we've experienced. These people died long before we got here, which meant Neoborax was at work long before we got here."

"What difference does that make to you?" Terri said.

"It means you didn't hire me so you could get started." Casey sounded angry. "You hired me so you could cover up that you already had."

In response, Terri shrugged.

With reverence and gentleness, Priya examined the bodies closer, focusing on the legs and heads. "There are significant genetic abnormalities here. The leg bones are bowed. Look at how misshapen the woman's jaw is."

Grant gave the woman's skull a closer look. He'd been taken aback by the shrunken skin, but now with Priya holding the head up, the jaw deformity was obvious. The front of the skull also had a pronounced, unhealthy slope to it. Her teeth barely met.

"I wonder how she chewed food?" Grant said.

"I'll bet the mortar and pestle against the wall were for her food," Priya said. "If I dared try to open their jaws, I bet the teeth would be a nightmare in all of them. Add in their diminished stature and these bodies show all the classic signs of inbreeding."

Crusher screwed his face up in disgust and stepped away from the corpses.

Terri turned to Crusher. "Search the rest of this village for anyone else, alive or dead."

Crusher looked relieved to get out of the room. "I'm okay finding neither."

"Inbreeding is a real danger in isolated societies," Priya continued. "The stronger tribes of this era encouraged inter-tribal marriage, though whether to stay robust or whether that practice made them robust, is up for debate."

"So these may have been the last members of the tribe that built these dwellings over a century ago?" Grant said.

"And Neoborax gassed them," Priya said. "Before we could have them pass on their history to us."

"What do you think they'd have told you?" Terri said. "They look a little, well, *mentally challenged* I think is the politically correct phrase."

"Even more reason to have left them alone, to live out their lives in the same place and the same manner as their ancestors. If Neoborax had made a proper survey of the canyon before blowing parts of it up, they would have discovered these poor people."

"Maybe they did," Casey said, "and they didn't care."

"Look," Terri said. "I didn't know anything about these buildings or these people in front of us. Not that it would have mattered. My job is to find recoverable uranium. The rest of this seems to be getting in the way of that job."

Grant could see this discussion was getting too heated. He opted to redirect it. "The mystery of this place that remains unsolved is why were these people still here? The canyon floor is dangerous and the tribe could have left when they saw their population dwindle or become genetically compromised."

"Now you're thinking like an anthropologist," Priya said.

"There's no need to be insulting," Grant said with a smile.

Priya smiled back.

"How could they even live up here anyway?" Kraus said. "How could they get food?"

"We found farming implements in that workshop," Casey said. "There are probably terraced plots along the cliff just as this village is."

Grant knelt down and ran his fingers across the woman's leather tunic. "This looks and feels like phytosaur skin, and there was a phytosaur skull in the workshop. They definitely made trips down to the canyon floor."

Kraus picked up a spear leaning against the wall. "You seriously think they took out dinosaurs with one of these?"

"More likely they scavenged a corpse," Grant said, "but the phytosaurs sure as hell didn't climb up here and shed their skin as an offering."

"All this guessing is pointless," Terri said. "All that matters is getting out of this canyon. If these people had a way down to the river, maybe they had a way up as well. We just haven't found it yet."

The group left the dead to care for themselves. Priya closed the door to their unintended tomb with respect. Grant went to the edge of the plaza and looked across the canyon. Down below, a pair of phytosaurs bellowed.

He certainly hoped there was a way up and out of here, because there was no way he was going down into that canyon again.

CHAPTER TWENTY-TWO

Crusher returned to the plaza and reported that there wasn't anyone else, living or dead, in the village. Then the group split back up to continue exploring the ruins. Grant took Priya back to the workshop he and Casey had discovered. The others searched the rest of the village.

Before they entered the room, Priya pointed past Grant. "What's that over there?"

Whatever it was, Grant and Casey hadn't noticed it. Priya wasn't waiting for his response anyway. She walked over to the edge of the plaza behind the building.

Near the corner sat a pile of rope pieces, pottery jugs, and the remains of what looked like a six-foot-high A-frame wooden structure. A shaft connected the two sides at the top with a grooved circular wheel on the shaft. A second wheel hung below the first.

Something smelled rank. Grant summoned the courage to lean over the edge for a better look. Along the cliff to his right, a precipitous channel had been cut into the rock, about three feet wide. It ran like a steep slide all the way to where the river cut into the cliff's base. The stones were stained red and yellow and the stink reminded Grant of an abandoned outhouse. He turned away and back to Priya.

The smell hadn't seemed to register with her at all. But she was fascinated by the A-frame device.

"What do you think that is?" Grant said.

"It's ingenious is what it is. Tell me, what's the biggest downside of living in this village in the sky?"

"Being one misstep away from plummeting to my death?"

"No," Priya said, irked. "Resupply. Everything you need is down in the canyon and you would have to haul it up those steps. This device kept you from having to do that. A rope used to run through this wheel here and all the way to the bottom."

Priya picked up a bit of the rope that had a loop tied in it. "Those pottery containers would be tied to the loop and brought up full of water or whatever was harvested from below."

"Not to sound dismissive—" Grant said.

"Which is what everyone being dismissive starts a sentence with."

"But," Grant continued, "that doesn't seem impressive. The rest of the world had steam engines and printing presses when this was made."

"But this society didn't even have the wheel. Yet they used the concept of the wheel to make a pulley, which is a huge innovation that makes work much easier. This kind of breakthrough hasn't been seen in native cultures. This village will yield more than meets the eye."

"Remind me to audit one of your classes next semester," Grant said. "And I'm afraid to ask about this sluice-looking thing over here."

"What's the one thing a society wouldn't want up in the village very long?"

Grant cringed. "Human waste?"

"Bingo. That is the equivalent of a sewer. Dump it all there, then wash it down with water brought up on the pulley."

"There's a cliff here," Grant said. "They could have just dumped it over the side."

"And it would splatter against the rocks, cook in the sun, attract creatures. Would you dump a chamber pot out of a sixth story window?"

"I see your point. It smells like that family was still using this thing."

"Despite the fact that for whatever reason they couldn't repair the broken pulley system to bring up the flushing water."

"For flushing water," Grant said, "even *I* would make the trip down and back."

Excitement lit up Priya's eyes. "These findings are as thrilling to me as the discovery of living dinosaurs are to you."

"Thrilling isn't the word I'd use," Grant said. "At least they're less likely to eat us alive."

Priya headed for the workshop. "Let's see what other surprises this place has in store for us."

As they entered the workshop, Priya sighed like she'd crossed through the gate to heaven. She glided from tool to tool, examining them, running a finger along their chipped surfaces. Several tanned sections of leather a few feet square lay on the table.

Priya pointed to them. "Phytosaur skin?"

Grant examined it. "Sure looks like it. Harvested off the dead, I'm guessing."

Priya stepped over to study the leather thongs and the knots that secured the stone blades to several implements.

"This is so exhilarating," she said. "These people were living in isolation for so long, this is like time traveling back to see how native tribes lived a thousand years ago."

"I used to dream of traveling back in time to see living dinosaurs," Grant said. "I've definitely crossed that off my bucket list."

Priya squinted at one of the spears. "The thongs tying some of these together are new, but none of the stone blades are, and most of them are quite dull. They would be difficult to use. It's possible that this last family still had the skill for the leather work, but no longer had the skill to chip themselves new arrowheads and hoe blades."

"Because no one taught them?"

"Or genetic decay made it impossible for them to understand the process anymore."

"Maybe it was the same situation with the broken water bucket system. I'll bet they didn't have any more of an understanding how this place was built than we do."

Priya glanced around the room one more time, then headed for the narrow stairs to the second floor. She scampered up them and Grant sighed. The slim steps would require a balancing act for him to get his much wider body to the top without falling. Now that he knew how short the people who lived here were, the small steps made sense, but appreciating them didn't make him happier about trying to ascend them.

Grant leaned hard into the wall as he climbed the stairs one delicate footfall at a time. The stone floor below was damn hard and unforgiving, and he had no interest in executing a belly flop on top of it.

"Doing okay?" Priya called down.

"Absolutely. I just like letting you make all the discoveries."

Grant eventually made it to the second floor. This room was as large as the one beneath it, but it was empty. While the lower room looked like it had been regularly swept, this one certainly had not. Tiny drifts of windblown sand covered the floor. Grant shuffled through some and then stared at the walls.

While the walls below had been barren, these were painted, but not with the crude artwork that had adorned the family's room. These were filled with square-shaped symbols, columns and columns of them, along with pictures between some.

The same forces of nature that had blown in the sand over the centuries had also done a job on the artwork. Missing flakes of paint gave the pictures a diseased look. In some spots larger patches were gone. Lower down on the wall the speckled remains of the paintings looked like they'd been subjected to sandblasting.

What looked like a huge map of the canyon carved into wood hung on the wall to the right.

Priya examined the map. "This board is solid mahogany. That grows in South and Central America. How could this wood get here?"

Next, she sidestepped over near the window where the light was brightest. Standing inches from the wall, she traced one symbol with the tip of her finger a fraction of an inch off the surface. Her jaw hung open.

"This village is an incredible find," she muttered. "It will rewrite history."

"What is all this on the walls?" Grant said.

"These symbols are a written language. It looks similar to what Aztec and Maya used, but it is definitely not the same. Another South American connection, like the mahogany. Native American tribes did not have written languages, but this tribe did. In a society without paper, like cavemen in earlier epochs, the people recorded what they wanted preserved on these walls. Indeed, what you are looking at is likely to be North America's first library."

"From a canyon floor perspective, it could also be North America's first example of cloud storage."

Priya didn't react to Grant's joke. The symbols on the wall now had her undivided attention. Grant went over to one of the pictures. It was of a phytosaur. The work was exceptionally realistic and accurate. In addition to losing the skill to make some tools, the village's last family also had let mastering the paint brush slip from their grasp as well.

Grant was still more amazed by the hanging map of the canyon. The contours were right and the proportions amazingly accurate considering these people had absolutely no technology to help them make it. A faded blue river ran down the center with the inlet and outlet marked. A good portion of the map's center details had succumbed to the elements.

"What's that down there?" Priya said, pointing at Grant's feet.

He'd moved enough sand to partially reveal a design carved into the stone, with a style like the phytosaur warning chiseled into the top of the steps.

"These people loved walking on artwork," Grant said.

Priya dropped to her hands and knees and began sweeping away the sand. Grant stifled a groan as he dropped down and joined her. In a few minutes they'd cleared away the center of the room.

They revealed a circular design with language glyphs all along the edge. Several concentric circles of other glyphs included sets of what looked like arrowheads pointing outward. In the center of the smaller circle was a face, although Grant thought it looked uncomfortably like a skull.

"This is a calendar," Priya said. "Very similar to the Mayan version. Using the sun and stars you can keep track of the date, and more importantly, count down to events like the summer and winter equinoxes. That's why there isn't anything in this room. It was kept empty to use the calendar."

"But it doesn't look like anyone's been using it," Grant said.

"Perhaps something else our last family standing didn't know how to use." Priya went back to study the glyphs on the wall.

"Do any of those symbols make sense to you?" Grant said.

"These glyphs here, these resemble the Aztec ones for duty and courage and time. I'm assuming the painting here similar to a lizard represents one of your phytosaurs."

Grant gave it a closer look. It was a lifelike dinosaur picture, but not of a phytosaur. This one was of a Coelophysis, the nimble predator whose fossilized skull Grant had seen down in the canyon.

"This painting isn't a phytosaur," Grant said, "and has too many correct details to be something one of these people imagined."

"Is it too much to ask that this one is a herbivore?"

"Not only was it a carnivore, it probably ate phytosaurs."

Sand caked a row of painted carvings in the wall beside the picture and Grant began to sweep one clean with the palm of his hand. He uncovered a carving similar in style to the one at the top of the stairs from the canyon. Traces of paint in the grooves and around the perimeter hinted at how impressive they must have been when first created.

"Ahh!" Priya rushed over and grabbed his hand. "Gently! You'll do more damage in a second than Nature has done in a hundred years."

Priya took a deep breath and blew more sand from the painting, then swept the more stubborn bits off with a caress of her fingertips. Grant mimicked her technique on the stone beside her. In a few minutes they'd uncovered a sequence of five pictures.

The first one showed people standing around what looked like a cave. A jumble of giant eggs covered the floor. Two figures were lifting one egg from the ground.

In the second picture, two people stood by a broken egg between two crossed palm trees. A dinosaur's head stuck from the open egg.

In the third picture, a Coelophysis stood atop a dead phytosaur lying on its back.

In the fourth picture, a number of people were walking up what looked like the stairway carved into the cliff. Each of them was carrying an egg.

"Wow," Priya said. "This is fascinating. It is common for a society without universal literacy to use pictures to tell stories and pass down knowledge. But rarely does one discover such a stunning example."

"These remind me of the storyboards for a film project of one of my novels," Grant said. "And that story had a bloody ending."

"These tell the people what they need to do," Priya said. "Like in many Mesoamerican cultures, high priests kept the calendar updated and then timed activities of the group by it. At a certain time, it seems that these people were to take an egg from a nest down to the canyon floor, and then hatch it."

Grant saw where this theory was going. "The calendar on the floor here probably timed the growth of the phytosaur population in the canyon. At the point where overpopulation would collapse the ecosystem, the villagers were supposed to set a predator free among them. The predator would cut back the population and then lay more eggs. The people would bring the new eggs to the nest so they could hatch the next annual, or biannual cycle, whichever it was."

"This is the owner's manual to Desolation Canyon, the instructions to keep it running." Priya looked concerned. "If my theory is correct, and until recently the mummified family was still following the practices…"

"Then somewhere in this cliff," Grant said, "there's a nest of eggs from one of the fiercest predators of the Triassic."

CHAPTER TWENTY-THREE

Terri wondered how much worse this situation could get.

She'd abandoned any hope of finding the mineable uranium that she'd promised to Neoborax. She was close to abandoning hope of even getting out of this canyon alive.

Climbing up the steps to this abandoned village initially felt like a relief. Anything closer to the canyon rim and further from rampaging dinosaurs was moving in the right direction. But once she'd arrived and found there was still fifty feet of overhanging rock between her and the rest of the world, she'd seen this place for what it was, a dead end. A rescue team was even less likely to find them up here, and while starvation would kill them slower than a dinosaur's jaws, it would inevitably kill them just the same.

Even if they were rescued, *all* rescued that is, that could make her situation even worse. When the story of this operation came out, Neoborax would disavow any knowledge that she'd been working on the company's orders. They'd all but told her that before she assembled her mercenary team.

There was no way in hell these three college professors would keep their mouths shut about what had happened in the canyon. They'd be shouting on social media about environmental violations, dead workers, and dinosaurs before Neoborax could even offer them a small fortune and a non-disclosure agreement.

She had no faith that sarcastic jerk Coleman would take even the most generous offer. She corrected herself. He'd take it, and then spill the beans anyway.

Terri wondered if she could even trust Kraus. He might try to dump all the blame in her lap to save his own skin. No, the only way to salvage this situation was for her to be the sole survivor. Neoborax alone would hear the story of what happened here, and the company would have only her undisputed version of it.

Coming out of here alone wouldn't be hard. She did have one of the only two guns among the group, not to mention that the cliffside plaza had no guard rails and accidents could happen. She just needed to make sure she got the maximum use out of each of these people before she dispatched them to the Great Beyond.

As the rest of the group split up to check out the village, she went to the last room in the set that lined the rear wall. Unlike the rest, this room had no window openings. In addition, this door was unique. The others had the simplest of mechanisms to keep them closed, just a small sliding piece of wood that went into the stone frame. In this kind of community, she guessed if you needed locks you were doomed.

This door had a crossbeam that ran across the opening, reminding her of the way the giant gates on Kong Island had been kept shut in that old movie. This setup wasn't to keep people out of the room, it was to keep something in.

She smiled. *Maybe the society had a jail because some people took advantage of all those unlockable doors.*

Terri lifted the crossbeam from the door. It felt much lighter than she'd expected. She thought maybe it was rotten on the inside. She set it aside and pushed open the door. It creaked on its leather hinges.

She stepped inside. The light from the open door revealed a shockingly large room. It stretched out at least fifty feet further into the side of the cliff. The walls and ceiling beyond the first ten feet of the room were completely natural. Also beyond that first ten feet of finished stone floor, the lumpy ground looked untouched, save for a smattering of gaps a few feet wide and at least as deep. It looked like this natural cave had already been here when this village had been built.

She set her rifle down in a corner of the room and pulled out a flashlight from her pack. Terri clicked it on and played the beam across the far wall. Crude steps climbed up to where they met the ceiling. A flaking painting of a two-legged dinosaur covered a flat spot in the surface there.

These people's choice of artwork stinks, she thought.

An anomaly in the cave wall then caught her eye. A wide band of bleached rock wrapped around the cavern about chest high, and below it was a black-green band like the ring on a filthy bathtub. A little surge of adrenaline passed through her.

If that deposit is pitchblende, she thought, *that deposit has uranium in it.*

She dropped her pack and dug the Geiger counter from the bottom, one of the many things in her pack she'd kept secret from the others, even Kraus. She marched across the uneven floor to the far end and took a reading for radioactivity with the meter.

The needle jumped. As with almost all naturally occurring uranium, the dosage was nothing for her to worry about, but it was enough to prove that this would be a very profitable vein to mine. Plus, it was close to the canyon rim for extraction, it was already exposed, and the idiots who lived here had already custom built a perfect work area outside the cave entrance.

Terri's future brightened like a rising sun. Once she showed this to Neoborax, all sins would be forgiven, all proof of them swept under the rug.

"Terri?" Priya called from the doorway.

Terri's heart jumped. She switched off the clicking Geiger counter and slid it back into her open backpack. The college contingent didn't need to know about this amazing find.

Terri scooped up her pack and started walking back to Priya. Grant stepped into the doorway. He looked around the cave and his face went white.

"Terri, don't move!" Grant said. "Those aren't rocks you're standing on. Those are dinosaur eggs."

CHAPTER TWENTY-FOUR

Grant's pulse raced as he looked across to Terri on the cavern's far side. He might love paleontology, but he was in no mood to observe a newly hatched Coelophysis right now.

"Dinosaurs lay eggs?" Terri said.

"Just like snakes do," Grant said. "But what's inside is even less cuddly."

Priya pointed up to the dinosaur painting near the ceiling. "Those eggs contain something a lot like that."

Kraus arrived in the doorway with Casey and Crusher in tow. "What's going on?"

"We're trying to keep Terri from getting us all eaten," Grant said. "She found a nest."

Casey's eyes went wide. "Those are phytosaur eggs?"

"No, these are Coelophysis eggs, because hey, why get trapped in a canyon with only *one* species of extinct, murderous dinosaur, right?" Grant turned to Terri. "Terri, try to walk in the lower, dirt-filled areas between the eggs. I'm not sure how hard the shells are, but there's no point in pushing our luck."

Terri slung her pack over one shoulder. On the tips of her toes, she began a slow, zig-zagging walk back to the stone floor. With every step, Grant anticipated hearing the crack of an egg and the hiss of a newly hatched predator. After an eternity of slow-motion hopscotch, Terri jumped across the last two feet of the nest and landed on the finished floor.

It sounded like the entire group exhaled at once. Terri dropped her pack on the ground and seemed to melt in relief.

"Grant, how do you know those are eggs?" Casey said.

"The room above the workshop you and I checked out was like a reference library for these people. There were paintings and glyphs all over the walls that described how these villagers used to tend dinosaur eggs. We were looking for the nest, but Terri had already found it."

"So what's keeping all these eggs alive?" Casey said. "And more importantly, what's keeping them from hatching right now?"

"A number of reptile species' hatching cycles are driven by temperature," Grant said. "The difference between the canyon floor and this underground area might be extreme enough to make that happen. But an annual cycle is a long time for an embryo in an egg to stay alive without getting some nutrients and energy."

Casey did a double take at the green-gray stratum along the cavern's back wall. He turned to Terri. "That's pitchblende, isn't it?"

A guilty look crossed Terri's face. "It looks like it."

"The energy keeping the eggs alive could come from the walls," Casey said. "Pitchblende can be loaded with uranium that could emit a low dose of radiation."

"Damn!" Crusher said as he backed up to the doorway.

"Not enough to hurt us," Casey said.

"But maybe enough to keep the Coelophysis eggs alive," Grant said.

"You read too many of your own silly monster books," Terri said. "Creatures adapted to live off radiation went out of style in the 1950s."

"There are deep sea creatures adapted to live off sulphur vents," Grant said. "Anything is possible. Sunlight lets us process Vitamin D and that's radiation. It's possible that our atmosphere millions of years ago let in far more radiation and these creatures took advantage of that through evolution."

"And why they seem to spontaneously expire," Priya said. "There are no instructions to the villagers on how to kill the Coelophysis once the phytosaur population is knocked down."

"And an unchecked hunter would naturally hunt prey to extinction," Grant said, "and then cause its own. Or perhaps once deprived of the radiation in here that keeps the eggs alive, the hatched creature might slowly die."

"And force the natives to retrieve the eggs so they can survive in the irradiated nest," Priya said.

"You're saying that this society that was here, built this village and stayed in the canyon because they wanted to preserve the creatures here?" Kraus said. "Seems a little altruistic."

"No more than our taking care of our national parks," Priya said. "It may also have been a more symbiotic relationship than we see now. Who knows?"

"The four people here were probably due to release one of the Coelophysis creatures about now," Grant said. "That's why the phytosaurs have gotten out of control. Maybe if your mining hadn't gassed them all to death—"

Kraus cut him off. "The point here is that a second kind of living dinosaur makes our situation worse."

"Not at all," Terri said. "Now we're closer to surviving this ordeal. We just need to set some of these coelo-whatevers loose on the dinosaurs down there. They kill what's been killing us. Then they die, and we can get back to where we know Neoborax will be looking for us, and back where we can have access to the food we left behind and the water from the river."

"Wait, wait," Grant said. "You're saying we're going to dig a live dinosaur egg out of that nest, carry it down a flight of stairs that makes a shark tank look safe, drop it off in a valley patrolled by phytosaurs, and then make it back before dinosaurs start slashing us and each other?"

"Not *we*, Professor." Terri picked up her rifle from against the wall. "*You're* going to do all that."

CHAPTER TWENTY-FIVE

"Me?" Grant said. "I'm certainly not the most qualified egg carrier here. I can't even fry one without breaking the yolk."

"You're right," Terri said. "You aren't the most qualified, just the most expendable. Priya reads the Indian writing, Casey knows the earth, Kraus and Crusher work for Neoborax. You only dig up bones."

For the second time on this trip, Grant stopped himself from telling someone that fossils weren't bones.

"Look, this whole interpretation we've made is half-guesswork," Grant said. "We don't even know if it's right."

"I'm sure my part of it is correct," Priya said.

"You aren't helping here," Grant said.

"Isn't that what you told me you scientists do?" Terri said. "Test hypotheses? You're about to test one. You should be excited."

"I am. I just naturally mask my excitement with a look of panic and dread. In fact, I'm so excited that the thrill of doing this may make me drop the egg and break it."

Terri pointed the rifle barrel at the nest. "There's more where that one came from. You three need to get digging."

"Threats aren't needed," Casey said. He turned to his colleagues. "This plan might work, and I can't think of another one anyway."

"There's the 'quietly starve to death in the village' plan," Grant said.

"There are digging tools in the workshop," Casey said. "I'll get them."

Casey headed over to the workshop.

"I wouldn't mind if Kraus gave us a hand," Grant said.

"I would," Kraus said.

Grant looked to Crusher. The man glared at him from under his hardhat. Seemed like digging was going to be a Robeson faculty team building exercise.

After a minute or two, Casey returned with a handful of the primitive tools. Priya gave them some coaching on how they were used and then the three professors went to one of the eggs near a hole, and began to clear away the dirt. Terri, Crusher, and Kraus retreated to the doorway and spoke in hushed whispers.

"Since we aren't sure what makes it hatch," Grant whispered, "I say we try not to smack it."

"I second that motion," Casey said.

Priya leaned in closer to Grant. "What is your plan?"

"Me? I don't have one. Since we've set foot in this giant reptile nightmare, have I looked like a man with a plan?"

"Just get the egg down there," Casey said, "and get back up here. If everything works the way you two think, there will be fewer dinosaurs to worry about, and a better chance we all survive."

"Do you think after everything Terri has done," Priya said, "she'll let us out of here alive?"

"We have to hope so," Casey said.

"Great," Grant said. "My survival depends on Terri the Grinch's heart growing three sizes at the end of the story. And to think I was worried."

They worked their way all around the egg. With the soil loosened and displaced, they were able to push the egg over into the open hole.

"It's lighter than I thought," Casey said.

Grant lifted the egg and groaned. "And still heavier than I'd hoped."

But the discovery did get him thinking about bone density and possible structural differences in Coelophysis from general dinosaurs. This line of scientific wondering was interrupted by a twinge of pain in his lower back. He set the egg down on the finished floor at the edge of the nest. Then he got out and stood beside it.

"And?" Terri said.

"Oh, you want me to take the egg down *now*? Okay, that part wasn't clear."

Grant knelt, wrapped his arms around the egg, and lifted. The egg had to weigh sixty pounds if it weighed an ounce.

"Let me help him with that," Casey volunteered.

"He'll have to manage it," Terri said.

"Thanks, Casey," Grant said as he leaned against the wall for a moment. "But there's no way two people could hold this thing at once, especially not going down those stairs."

Inside the egg, something stirred. Grant nearly dropped the thing in shock. "Whatever's in here is already saying it wants to come out."

"Then you should stop wasting time," Terri said. "Crusher, follow him, make sure he gets the egg safely to the canyon floor. Kraus, give him your rifle."

"You got it." Kraus slid his rifle from his shoulder and handed it to Crusher.

Crusher looked alarmed at this turn of events. "Hey, Kraus is probably a better shot than I am."

"You'll be so close you don't have to aim," Terri said. "Go."

Crusher sighed and stepped up behind Grant.

"If you want to go first," Grant said, "I'm fine with that."

"Get moving," Crusher growled.

Grant flexed his already complaining biceps and hoisted the egg to under his chin. He lumbered out of the nest room and over to the stairs. Carrying the egg promised to make the difficult task of going down the steps seem closer to suicidal. The thought "Better me than Priya" passed through his mind, and then he realized the nimbler Priya might actually do a better job.

One step at a time, he descended the short, first flight to the observation patio. As he set both feet on the patio, he sighed in relief.

That wasn't so bad, he thought. *I can do this.*

He carried the egg over to the next set of steps and looked down. Grant swore they had narrowed since he'd last seen them. It also seemed like someone had added a hundred steps to the staircase.

Update, he thought. *There's no way I can do this.*

He glanced down at his feet to make sure he hit the first step. The warning carving of the man being attacked by a dinosaur was beside his foot.

"Thanks for the heads-up, thousand-year-dead ironic artist," Grant said.

"We don't have all day," Crusher said from the other side of the patio.

"Of course," Grant said. "How could I forget that we all have facials scheduled for later on? Say, that rifle looks pretty heavy. I'll swap with you if you want a break."

"You don't get going, something will be broken, all right."

Grant began the slow, uneasy return to the canyon floor. Each step sent the weight of the giant egg in a different direction, and demanded Grant rebalance himself against it. His waddling descent alternated between crashing one shoulder into the rough face of the cliff and trying not to topple over the open side of the stairs.

"Damn," Crusher said. "Could you be any slower?"

"As a matter of fact, I could. Let me put some effort into that."

"Keep moving, smart-ass."

The dinosaur in the egg squirmed again. Grant threw himself against the cliff wall to fight the weight shift. The creature's movement was much stronger than before, and this time the sound of scraping within the shell accompanied it.

Grant's heart jumped. No part of that was at all comforting. The last thing he needed was this egg cracking open and him holding a newborn apex predator.

He resumed his descent, now faster than he thought safe. Bruises were already swelling on his pounded left shoulder. Each hurried step sent a spray of sand and pebbles off the side of the steps and plummeting to the canyon floor.

Grant's hands began to sweat. His grip on the eggshell slipped.

"Hell no," he whispered. He hugged it tighter to keep from dropping it.

With a dozen steps left to go, a new noise came from within the egg. At the narrow end, right below his chin, came the sharp smack of bone against shell. The paleontologist part of him thought *Wow, I'm going to see how a Coelophysis hatches.*

The panicked rest of him dope-slapped the paleontologist part. Terror sent Grant scrambling down the last few steps.

Once at the base of the stairway, he remembered the circle of stones halfway to the river with the crossed palm trees. That spot was a dead ringer for the egg-hatching location in the wall painting. He wondered if the hatching egg needed to be in that location for some reason. Grant nursed a hope that it was because the rocks were magic and protected the egg deliverer from being eaten by the baby Coelophysis. He was fresh out of rational things to hope for.

He carried the egg down the trail.

"Hey, where are you going?" Crusher said.

"Dinosaur maternity ward is down here."

Crusher gave the undergrowth a wary look, then took a seat on the steps. "Terri said make sure you got the egg to the canyon. You did. I'll wait here."

Grant continued on and made it to the circle of stones. In a wheezing shuffle he stepped into the center and let the egg roll out of his arms. The stone circle was very coincidentally egg-sized.

Between the exertion of trundling down the stairs, and a lack of real food, the sudden bending over to drop the egg made his head swim. Everything around him got blurry. He took a knee by the egg to keep from falling over. Grant gave it a soft pat.

"Good boy," he whispered.

Something that sounded like a thunderclap snapped in Grant's left ear. His vision re-focused and he looked up to see a quarter-inch wide crack at the top of the egg.

CHAPTER TWENTY-SIX

Grant rose to his feet, still unsteady, and began to back away.

The crack in the egg grew like a big zipper, straight down the side. The shell split into two halves, then crumbled into smaller pieces. It revealed a green, egg-shaped mass inside a clear, glistening sack.

Grant's heel hit a rock. It caught his foot and he fell back on his butt.

The sack tore open. The Coelophysis that had been inside looked like it had been folded up and compressed. With closed eyes, the head lifted from the mass and shook off the sloppy remains of the sack. Then the rest of the creature stretched out. A long tail unwound itself and then slapped the ground behind the creature. Lower and then upper limbs expanded. A little Coelophysis stood in the middle of the stone circle.

This isn't bad, Grant thought. *It's a baby, no taller than a sandhill crane. It must take years to mature to full size.*

The dinosaur opened its mouth and took a huge first breath.

It was like compressed air filling a balloon. The creature expanded in every direction. The oxygenation had triggered some kind of intense cell growth. Suddenly, it was as tall as Grant.

Grant rose to his feet, trying like hell to stay silent.

Maybe it will open its eyes and imprint on the first creature it sees, Grant thought. *That will be me, and it will never hurt its foster dad.*

The creature's eyes opened. They focused on Grant and then narrowed. The creature hissed and a thick, black forked tongue flapped in its open jaws. The Coelophysis took one unsteady step forward.

Grant realized that the only thing Junior had just imprinted on was its first meal.

Grant spun around and ran for the stairs. The dinosaur hissed again and branches snapped as it began its pursuit.

Grant's whole body already ached from carrying the egg down the cliff. He felt like he was running in slow motion for the stairs. Junior was stretching muscles for the first time, so Grant prayed it wasn't doing much better.

Grant broke out of the trees to find Crusher standing just a few steps up from the canyon floor. Crusher must have heard the Coelophysis' hissing. He already had the rifle at his shoulder, pointed in Grant's direction.

Grant prayed that he was pointing past Grant and at the creature. This definitely did not need to be one of those situations where out of mercy, one guy shoots another to save him from a grisly death.

Crusher's aim did not waver.

The sound of armored skin and claws against dirt came from close behind Grant. The creature hissed again, this time louder and angrier.

Crusher fired.

Grant's foot snagged a root. This time he hit the ground hard and face first. Dirt speckled his glasses. He looked over his shoulder and hoped to see a dinosaur paused and clutching a fatal wound.

The bullet had made no difference. The newborn Coelophysis had closed to within feet of Grant. In two strides it was at Grant's heels.

Then it leapt, straight over Grant. As he looked up at the underside of the dinosaur, bits of the slimy egg sack splattered his face. The predator sailed past, and landed right in front of Crusher.

Crusher didn't have time to fire a second shot. The dinosaur bit off his head like a kid devouring an ear off a chocolate bunny. The Coelophysis swallowed as Crusher's headless body tumbled off the steps. The creature bent down, bit the corpse around the waist, and shook it. Then the dinosaur tossed it a few yards away, as if to confirm that the man was indeed dead.

The Coelophysis jogged over to Crusher's corpse and straddled him with its back to the stairs. With the same motion as a chicken pecking at the ground, it began to chomp and swallow bits of the body.

Grant's slowing pulse stopped pounding in his ears. He realized he had two options. First, lie here and hope the satiated Coelophysis wandered off for a nap after eating. Second, he could hope that the distracted dino wouldn't notice as he crawled over to and then up the stairs.

Both options were awful, both seemed doomed to fail. But the idea of lying here with his eyes closed while the creature swallowed and slurped Crusher's corpse made the first option the least appealing. Plus, the anticipation of inactively waiting to be eaten would probably drive him nuts. He settled on option two.

Grant focused on the base of the stairs and began a quiet crawl. Afraid to lift his body up and gain the creature's attention, he kept his chest to the ground and moved forward with his arms and legs at his sides. This stance earned him a mouth full of dirt, so he raised himself up an inch or so.

Sharp pebbles dug into his hands and knees with every motion. From behind him came the crunch of bones as the dino devoured Crusher. The smell of blood and offal rolled across to him and foreshadowed his own doom. He kept his eyes on the steps, his roiling stomach in check, and tried to remember to breathe.

A few feet away lay Crusher's dropped rifle. Blood and organs covered most of it. Grant reasoned that dragging it through the dirt would slow him down even more and the rifle hadn't stopped Junior on its first try. Plus, he didn't want to touch it. He skipped the disgusting side trip.

A glance back confirmed the dinosaur was still feeding. Grant did a double take. It wasn't his imagination. The thing was larger. If the oxygen had turbocharged its growth, this first meal was supercharging it. Grant did not want to be anywhere near it whenever the creature peaked.

When his fingers finally touched that bottom step, the anticipation of getting out of here almost overwhelmed him. He struggled against the impulse to race up the steps. He reminded himself that he hadn't been in up-the-steps-racer form since his undergrad days, if then.

Grant began a slow, painful crawl up the steps. His stomach scraped across every edge. Each grip on a stone seemed to sand the tips of his fingers. His knees cracked against rock and he imagined a set of crutches in his near future. He alternated between a look up the stairs to judge his next handholds and then a sideways glance to see if his dinosaur was still occupied.

He wondered how high the thing could jump, and when it would be safe to get up and walk the rest of the steps. If this process hadn't been so painful, he'd have been glad to keep crawling until he was all the way back to the nest room.

He looked up at the steps, sighed, then back at the backside of the feeding dinosaur. Back to steps. Back to dino butt. Steps. Dino butt.

Wow, I may survive this, he thought.

Steps. Dino teeth.

The Coelophysis had finished off Crusher. Swaths of blood streaked the sides of its face. It had turned its head back to the stairs, and now had its eyes locked on Grant.

Grant froze. *Maybe it doesn't see me. If I stay perfectly still...*

Without taking its gaze from Grant, the dinosaur pivoted its body to face him. It opened its mouth and roared.

"Oh, hell."

Adrenaline blasted through his veins. He jumped up and took the steps two risers at a leap.

In two bounds, the dinosaur hit the bottom of the stairs. Grant's pounding heart threatened to crack his ribs if it didn't explode first. He covered another set of steps.

The Coelophysis jumped. Grant was much higher than Crusher had been, but so was the dinosaur's leap. It was aimed right for Grant.

Then gravity saved Grant's life. The dinosaur fell short. Its head struck the steps just below Grant's feet and took out two of them with a crash. It tumbled back to the ground, landed on its back, and rolled over onto its feet again. It gave its head a clearing shake.

Grant kept climbing. The dinosaur looked up at his retreating figure, cocked its head as if judging the distance, and seemed to guess it was too great. It turned and bounded away into the trees.

Grant made it to the observation patio and collapsed on the top step. Next to him was the carved dinosaur warning.

Grant patted it. "Still a hundred percent true."

CHAPTER TWENTY-SEVEN

Casey and Priya dashed down from the village and knelt beside Grant.

"We were watching from the village," Casey said. "That was close."

"Are you okay?" Priya said.

"Except for aging ten years in ten minutes," Grant said, "I'm doing peachy. Much better than Crusher."

"What happened to him was horrible," Priya said.

"It didn't take long for that thing to hatch," Casey said.

Grant cleaned the mess from his glasses. "No, it started moving in the egg as soon as we took it away from the uranium. The tribe had built a stone hatching circle down there, likely the minimum safe distance where they could drop the egg and get back up the stairs before hatching. The egg was already cracking before I got there."

"The native people probably got the eggs down the steps faster than you did," Priya said.

"I'm too tired to take that as an insult."

Kraus and Terri arrived. Terri looked furious. "Why did that thing jump over you to get to Crusher?" she said.

"Yes, I'm fine, Terri," Grant said. "Thanks for asking. Maybe it attacked Crusher first because he was shooting at it."

"From my angle it looked like he was shooting at you," Casey said.

"Seemed like a possibility to me as well."

"And you left my rifle down there?" Kraus said.

"It was coated in a B-grade horror movie level of blood, so I left it there. It's at the bottom of the stairs if you want it."

"It wasn't my imagination," Priya said, "that that thing got very big very fast."

"I can tell you from an uncomfortably close perspective it sure did," Grant said. "Oxygen and then protein let the creature compressed in that egg quickly swell to a much larger size. If it hadn't been ready to kill me, I'd have thought the evolutionary trait pretty amazing."

"So now we wait," Terri said. "The raptor-looking thing just has to eat its way through the crocodile-looking things."

"How long will that take?" Kraus asked.

"Depends on how hungry it is," Grant said. "But that growth spurt took a lot of energy, so I'd say it's hungry."

"The thing may also kill for the sport of it," Casey said. "It went after you with a full belly."

"I can look back at the glyphs and the calendar," Priya said, "and see if those have any clues about the duration."

"Not today you won't," Terri said. "It will be dark soon, and I have the only working flashlight. We'll sleep in the village rooms."

"I call one of the rooms that doesn't have four dead bodies or dinosaur eggs in it," Grant said.

"Spread yourselves out." Terri handed her rifle to Kraus. "You keep a watch on the observation patio. I'm not so sure that damn thing we hatched can't climb back up those stairs. If it tries, blast the steps out from underneath it."

"Roger that," Kraus said. "If I can see it coming in the dark."

"There are pottery shards all around the village," Casey said. "We can set them out on the steps. The creature will either slip on them or crunch them. Either way you'll hear a noise."

"I like that idea," Terri said.

"I hope that thing has grown too big to scale the steps," Priya said.

"I hope it prefers the taste of phytosaurs over humans," Grant said.

***

The group split up and into separate rooms. Priya took the second story records room, and Grant was glad she picked the spot that would be hardest for the Coelophysis to get to if it did manage to scale the stairs. Casey took the workshop below her. Grant and Terri ended up in separate rooms in the complex along the wall, between the nest room and the impromptu mortuary at the end.

As darkness fell, Grant gnawed at one of the miserable protein bars. All the people who said food was just fuel and the type unimportant had never been forced to eat these awful things. He vowed to live through this experience, not because he wanted to expose the crimes Terri and Neoborax had committed, but to savor a cheeseburger with a huge side of hot, crispy onion rings.

Grant had good reasons to hope for a better night's sleep tonight than last night. First, even a hard stone floor was better than rocky, uneven earth. Second, he wasn't worried about a phytosaur stomping him in his sleep. Third, his near misses with death had physically exhausted him.

But it wasn't to be. Every bump and bruise his body had absorbed all day seemed to announce its displeasure as he lay on the ground. He did doze in fits and starts for a while, but always haunted by dreams of dismemberment and being devoured by the canyon's dinosaurs. When he finally fell into a sound sleep, he was almost immediately awakened by the sound of a man's scream.

Grant jumped up off the floor and went to the window opening. He put on his glasses, which proved to be a wasted effort. It was like looking into an abyss out there. With the overhanging cliff, he could not even see the stars.

Grant went to use his phone as a flashlight. As expected, the battery was long dead. He opened the door and stepped out into the darkness. If someone was hurt, maybe he would stumble into them before he stumbled off the edge of the village. He made his way down the plaza with one hand on the side of the building.

The door beside his opened. A flashlight clicked on and Terri stepped out. The sight of Grant startled her and she shined the light in his face.

"It's Grant," he said as he shielded his eyes.

"Did you scream?"

"Not since this afternoon."

From over at the workshop, a light blinked on. It bobbed up and down and came closer to Grant and Terri. It was Priya, with her cellphone flashlight.

"I think the scream came from the observation patio," Terri said. "Follow me."

Terri began to jog across the plaza. Grant and Priya tried to keep up.

"Your phone still has a charge?" Grant said to Priya.

"I shut it off as soon as we saw there was no signal at the camp. Didn't you?"

"I won't dignify the question with an answer."

The three arrived at the top of the steps to the observation patio. Casey stood there. His skin looked especially white in the harsh flashlight beam.

"Did you scream?" Terri said.

"No, I heard it though. It sounded like Kraus. I left the workshop and managed to get this far, but without a light, I wasn't going to try and find the stairs."

"Kraus!" Terri called out. "Kraus!"

There was no answer.

"All of you stay here," she said.

For once Grant had no objection to following one of Terri's orders. The three professors waited as Terri descended the steps.

"Did you see anything out here?" Casey asked Grant.

"Nothing. I heard the scream, but it's damn near lightless out here."

From the plaza's edge, the three watched Terri's flashlight bounce and sweep across the patio as she called out for Kraus. The flashlight beam illuminated the steps heading down to the canyon. The minefield of pottery shards hadn't been touched.

Terri returned to the plaza. "Kraus isn't there. The rifle's also gone. Nothing came up the steps and grabbed him."

"Maybe something else grabbed him," Casey said. "Just because we only know of two dinosaurs in this canyon, that doesn't mean there aren't others, others that are nocturnal."

"The odds on there being one extinct species are poor," Grant said. "I'd say the odds of there being two in this small an area were impossible if I didn't know it was true. Three just can't happen."

"You can't see your hand in front of your face without a light," Priya said. "Maybe he fell off the edge."

"Or part of it collapsed," Casey said.

Terri gritted her teeth. "Whatever happened, we'll figure it out in the morning. Someone needs to keep an eye out here with Kraus gone."

Grant already knew where this conversation was going. "Gee, do I get to volunteer for that?"

"As a matter of fact, I already volunteered you."

"But you don't have a rifle to back you up anymore."

Terri drew the big knife from the sheath on her belt. She laid it across the base of Grant's neck. "Do you think I need a rifle?"

"Well, no, as long as you're asking so nicely."

"Everyone else back to sleep." Terri put the knife back in its sheath. "We have a lot to sort out tomorrow."

The group climbed the steps. At the top, Grant slumped down on the plaza edge. Casey stayed behind as the others returned to where they had been sleeping.

"There are some rudimentary weapons in the workshop," Casey said. "You want me to bring you one?"

"For defense against dinosaurs or Terri?"

"Maybe both?"

"Nothing in that Neolithic arsenal would defend me against either of them."

"It is three to one now, and no guns on her side," Casey said. "We could make a go of it against her."

"We'd aim to subdue her," Grant said, "but she'd have no second thoughts about killing one of us. That's no way to go into a fight. One or all of us are bound to get hurt. Let's just see what unfolds."

"Okay. Stay awake out here."

"I'll brew up a pot of coffee."

Casey disappeared into the darkness. Grant looked out over the observation patio. Priya was right. He couldn't see his hand in front of his face. Which meant he couldn't see a Coelophysis in front of his face either.

He was sitting on guard duty with just his senses of hearing and smell to work with. He wasn't a guard dog as much as he was a canary in a coal mine. Everyone would know there was trouble as soon as he died.

Grant looked to his watch, knowing there was no way he could read the face. He wondered how long it would be until dawn.

CHAPTER TWENTY-EIGHT

"Nice job guarding us all!"

Terri's shout in Grant's ear awakened him immediately. He lay on the plaza near the steps. He winced and sat up. Terri's red face glowered at him.

"If you're taking breakfast orders," Grant said, "I'm in the mood for waffles."

Terri stormed past him and down the steps to the observation point. Grant stood up and the best he could initially manage was a stoop. Yesterday's injuries and a night on cold stone had done a number on his back. He moaned as he straightened up.

Terri went directly to the edge of the observation point. She looked down, shook her head, and whispered a curse as Grant came up beside her. At the bottom of the cliff lay Kraus' body.

"How could he have been so stupid?" Terri said. "It was pitch black for God's sake. You stay away from the edge."

Grant kicked the toe of his shoe against a jagged edge of the patio. Rock crumbled and rolled down into the canyon. "Maybe he was further away than you think. Any of these jagged spots could have collapsed with him on it."

"He didn't need to walk around. All he had to do was sit and listen. And now I've gone from two rifles to zero and everyone still alive is this side of useless."

"Careful," Grant said. "Such flattery might go to my head."

Terri stepped up inches from Grant's face. Her cheeks were flushed, her eyes aflame with anger. "The more you piss me off, the more likely you'll have an accident and end up on the canyon floor yourself."

Grant could see the general situation and his sarcasm had pushed Terri to the limit, and he was certain her threat wasn't at all idle. He stepped back.

Terri seemed to take that as a victory, and climbed the steps back to the plaza. She passed Casey and Priya, who joined Grant.

"She looks pissed off," Casey said. "So she must have been talking to you."

"That and seeing Kraus dead on the canyon floor ruined her mood. It looks like he just fell. You can take my word for it without having to see it."

"I don't know whether to be more afraid of her or the dinosaurs," Priya said.

"The dinosaurs are more predictable," Grant said.

From down in the valley came the anguished cry of a phytosaur. Near the river a set of trees swayed back and forth.

"Looks like the Coelophysis is doing its job," Casey said. "Every dinosaur it kills is one less that could kill us."

"How will we know when we can go back down?" Priya said.

Another phytosaur scream sounded, then was cut short. The trees stopped moving.

"When we stop hearing things like that," Grant said.

***

Terri was still livid when she returned to the room where she'd slept. Just when she'd thought she might be able to salvage this mess, it all went even further to hell. Stupid Kraus had to walk himself off a cliff. She was tempted to hike down to the canyon floor just to kick his corpse in frustration.

Her situation here wasn't tenable. These three eggheads would eventually do the math and see that they outnumbered her. Individually, she could bounce any of them off a wall, but three at once would be too much, not that there wouldn't be injuries all around for making the attempt. They might even try something while she was asleep and subdue her without a fight. Then when rescue came, it would be their story first, her story second, and she'd really be screwed.

The frustration of having climbed so close to the rim and not being able to get there came back to haunt her.

Why hadn't these people built a skylight into this place? she thought.

An idea came to her. She could make a skylight herself.

She hadn't told the others, but she had the remaining explosives in her backpack and the means to set them off. The nest room had steps to the ceiling where the dinosaur was carved into the stone. A charge there would weaken the ceiling enough that the weight of it would probably cause a partial collapse. Then she could climb right the hell out of this nightmare and start walking back to the worksite along the dinosaur-free rim where rescuers were bound to arrive.

She realized an added bonus. The rich vein of uranium in the nest room would be even easier to get to.

Terri smiled. As the sportscasters liked to say, she would be snatching victory from the jaws of defeat. She'd also be snatching herself away from the jaws of dinosaurs. Once she figured out how to leave the three professors in the danger zone while she set the charge off from a safe spot, she'd have a foolproof plan.

But step one was to set up the charge without anyone knowing. She laughed as she thought how easy that would be. None of those cowering college professors were going into the nest room, that was for sure.

She grabbed her pack and slung it over her shoulder. A quick glance out the window told her the plaza was empty. The other three were still on the observation point.

Excellent, she thought.

Terri left her room and went straight for the nest room. She took one more quick glance back to be certain she was still unobserved, then entered the room and closed the door behind her.

She clicked on her flashlight. The sight was unnerving now that she knew those little mounds in the floor were dinosaur eggs. But she calmed herself knowing that the same radiation that made this place valuable to Neoborax would keep the dinos sleeping in their eggs. The collapsed roof would crush the eggs or bury them deeper. Either way, she'd give the Neoborax team a heads-up and they'd be prepared for the creatures with overwhelming firepower.

Terri shined the light on the far wall and the steps that led up to the painting. She'd be able to reach the ceiling easily from there, and it would be a perfect place to set the charges.

She'd been promised a bonus based on how well the mine paid out. This was going to be a big score for her. She wondered how many zeros there would be on her check.

Terri opened the top to her backpack. One of the explosive charges was right on top. She raised an eyebrow. The detonator was already set in the charge.

And that was the last thought Terri Nagle would ever have.

CHAPTER TWENTY-NINE

Grant was speaking to Casey and Priya on the observation patio when the plaza behind them erupted in a fireball and a thunderous boom.

The plaza beneath his feet vibrated. Grant covered his face with his hands as a shotgun blast of tiny rocks and sand swept the observation point. The debris nailed Casey and Priya hard in their backs. The concussion nearly knocked him off his feet.

The dust settled and everyone turned to face the plaza. A brown cloud enveloped the far corner. The three of them slowly made their way up the steps and stood on the plaza's edge.

"Terri?" Casey called out.

There was no response.

The settling dust revealed the explosion's origin, the blown-out wall of the nest room. If Terri had been anywhere near that room, Grant was sure she was dead.

"How could this happen?" Priya said.

"Casey," Grant said, "could that have been a kind of natural gas explosion?"

"It's possible. The same fissures that released that poisonous gas could have also tapped a pocket of natural gas. Any kind of spark, no matter how small, near a concentrated amount of gas, and, BOOM!"

"We need to find Terri," Priya said.

Given the condition Grant was sure Terri was in, he was certain he didn't *need* to find her at all. He'd already seen one dead body today and that was one over his personal limit.

But Casey and Priya moved toward the nest room, and Grant reluctantly followed.

"For the record," Grant said, "going toward the source of any explosion is against my better judgment."

The others ignored him. His first impulse was to hang back and await their report, but he doubted that would sit well in Priya's eyes. He kept pushing on.

A large crack ran through the plaza. It made a jagged line to the obliterated wall of the nest room. The room next door hadn't fared any better.

Grant arrived to find a blackened hole in the floor inside where the door had been. Bits of cloth, flesh, and Terri's backpack seemed to be everywhere.

"Oh my God," Priya said.

Grant followed her eyes and saw Terri's head over in the corner. He looked away immediately.

"This doesn't look like a natural gas explosion." Grant pointed to the charred hole in the floor. "The detonation looks like it happened—"

The sound of a cracking eggshell cut his sentence short. Grant caught his breath. He scanned the nest for the breaking shell.

Multiple eggs had cracks in them. The effects of the explosion had broken most of the eggs in the nest.

Then those eggs began to quake.

"I've already seen this movie," Grant said. "You won't like the ending."

On one of the nearby eggs, a several-inch-square fragment broke away. A Coelophysis eye stared out at them.

"Run!" Casey said.

The three turned and sprinted from the room. They headed for the observation point and the stairs to the canyon floor.

The plaza rumbled. Earth and stone ground together. Ahead of them, the crack across the plaza widened. The cliffside edge of the farther section shifted down. That half of the plaza floor stopped with a dangerous-looking downward angle. A stone rolled down it and sailed off the cliff.

Grant was in no mood to take a slide down those pavers and follow that stone. He skidded to a stop along with the others. He looked for another safe haven. The only option was in the opposite direction, toward the workshop and library at the plaza's far end.

Grant pointed at the structure. "In there!"

To their right, the entire nest room seemed to have come alive. Shattering eggs sent a snowstorm of shell fragments out onto the plaza. Coelophysis heads and upper bodies went erect out of the floor like awful blooming flowers. The cavern walls amplified the cries and hisses of the newly hatched and broadcast the sound out across the plaza.

Priya and Casey sprinted for the building. Grant executed more of a panicked jog. The three stepped over the broken door, entered the workroom, and ducked behind the wall.

"Having a door here would be nice," Priya said.

Casey pointed at Grant. "Blame Samson, here, for that."

Priya peered out the window opening. "Oh, my God."

Grant looked over her shoulders. There were at least a dozen newly hatched dinosaurs standing around the remains of the nest room. They stretched and sniffed the air. One broke for the far end of the plaza. It jumped the crack between the two sections, then completed an awkward scramble across the angled plaza with its claws scraping stone. At the far edge, it hopped off to the observation platform.

"Seems they know the food is down in the canyon," Casey said.

Two more dinosaurs jumped out of the nest. One took a deep breath and expanded to be much larger than the other. It immediately dove on its brother and pinned it to the ground. With one dart of its head it clamped its jaws around the wriggling dinosaur's neck, and severed the creature's head.

"Some don't want to travel that far for a first meal," Grant said.

"That's so bizarre," Priya said.

"It's a relatively common thing for predators. Makes sure the strongest survive."

Now the dinosaur hatching started full speed. The nest seemed like a pile of writhing, stretching, screaming Coelophyses. Spurts of blood and the crunch of bones told the story of many turning cannibal. Dinosaurs leapt from the fray and charged across the plaza on the way to the canyon.

One of the animals paused just before the crack in the plaza. It turned and sniffed the air in the direction of the work room.

"Uh oh," Grant said.

The dinosaur lowered its head and charged for the building.

"Upstairs," Grant said. "Now!"

He turned to see the other two were already at the base of the stairs and heading up.

Grant had just made it to the stairs when the dinosaur slammed through the doorway. It aimed straight for Grant. Grant backed up to the wall. The creature's head darted for him, jaws open.

The jaws stopped inches from Grant's head. The creature hissed and hot breath blasted Grant. Stinking dinosaur spittle landed on his face. The head jerked back and forth but got no closer. Grant looked past it and saw the dinosaur's hips stuck in the narrow doorway.

With his back to the wall, Grant scrambled up the steps to the second floor. The others waited breathlessly at the top.

"It can't get through the doorway," Grant said. "Finally, I'm the one who can make a fat joke."

Stone exploded downstairs. The dinosaur's head appeared at the base of the steps. It had smashed through the doorway.

"No way that doorway was up to code," Grant said.

The dinosaur roared and angled its head up the staircase. Its forked, black tongue licked the air. The opening to the second floor was wider than the doorway. This wasn't going to end well.

"Help me over here!" Priya shouted.

Grant saw she was standing next to the wooden map on the wall. Casey ran to the other side of it. They lifted it up and carried it to the stairway. Grant stepped aside and they dropped it over the hole. It landed with a thud and covered most of the opening.

Grant prayed that the "out-of-sight-out-of-mind" concept worked on a Coelophysis.

The dinosaur roared below them. The map jumped in the air, bumped up by the dinosaur's head. It landed back over the hole.

"That map isn't heavy enough to hold that thing back," Grant said.

Casey looked at Grant, then at the map board, then back to Grant. "Needs to be heavier."

"Now you're doing the fat joke?" Grant said.

"It will take all of us," Casey said. "C'mon."

The three of them dropped on top of the map board. Just as they did, the dinosaur slammed it again. The board rose an inch and dropped back down. Grant felt the impact from the base of his spine to the top of his head.

The Coelophysis roared its frustration. From downstairs came the crash of wood and stone as Grant imagined the furious beast smashing against the walls and whipping its tail through everything in the workshop.

Cracks ran up the sides of the library walls.

The dinosaur struck the bottom of the map board again, this time harder. Wood splintered and the board jumped high enough that the landing jarred Grant's teeth. The dinosaur pounded around the workshop again and the building shook.

The wall cracks expanded. Another one spread across the floor like a slow-motion lightning bolt.

Grant gripped the sides of the board. For the first time in his life, he wished he was fatter.

From below came the thud of dinosaur feet, as if somehow the creature was getting a running start. Then its head slammed into the map board again. This time the force was too great. The map board flipped sideways, spilling all three professors across the floor and into the far corner. The map board hit the floor beside them.

The dinosaur's head rose up from the stairway. It pivoted until it locked its eyes on the three in the corner. The creature roared and climbed the stairs.

Its shoulders rose and its smaller forelimbs reached up and grabbed the floor. As they helped pull its weight up the steps, the pressure on the floor widened the crack. Multiple new cracks raced up the walls. The entire building shuddered.

The floor began to sag. Grant grabbed the map board and pulled it up over the three of them. The others grabbed it like a shield.

Then the second floor collapsed. It dropped and pancaked the first floor with a crash. Grant bounced as it hit and held tight to the map board. The walls around them fell outward and the thin roof disintegrated. Adobe and dirt pummeled the map board. The load increased and started to press hard into Grant's chest. With a few more pounds, he was sure his ribs would break.

Then the rain of masonry stopped. Everything went quiet.

"Push!" Grant managed to wheeze out.

The three of them pushed against the map board. Grant and Casey's side rose higher, and the debris covering it slid off sideways. Grant sucked a few gallons of air into his freed lungs. Casey gave his side an extra heave and the board flipped off the trio.

"Anyone hurt?" Grant said.

Casey and Priya each did some form of a self-diagnostic and said no. Everyone got to their feet. Grant wiped his glasses with the sleeve of his shirt which barely made his view any clearer.

A pile of rubble buried the Coelophysis. Its snout poked out from under the debris. Blood trickled from its mouth, but it didn't move.

"That was lucky," Priya said.

"Better lucky than good is my personal motto," Grant said.

From the nest area came the cries of more new hatchlings. Several jumped from the nest and focused their attention on the three dusty professors.

"We aren't out of the woods yet," Casey said.

"But we *are* out of hiding places," Grant said.

The section of the plaza between them and the stairs to the canyon now looked like a slide pointed to the canyon floor. There was no crossing that.

The ground underneath them shifted.

"That building was part of the structural support for the plaza," Priya said. "This whole village won't last long."

"With my luck it will last long enough for the dinosaurs to eat us," Grant said.

The hatchlings took tentative steps toward the party and hissed.

"We have to get out of here," Casey said.

"Access to the steps is gone," Grant pointed to the edge of the plaza. "That leaves us the one-step staircase right there."

"There's another way." Priya took off before Grant could ask what she was talking about. She sorted through the rubble and pulled out three of the large leather squares they'd admired before.

Then Grant and Casey followed her around the rubble to the far edge of the plaza. They crouched down behind the last remaining wall of the workshop.

Priya pointed to the waste chute carved in the cliff side. "This goes down to the river."

"You want me to slide down the poop chute?" Grant said. "I've been told my novels are crap, but I don't think that means that I—"

"She's right," Casey said. "We're out of options."

Priya handed each of them a leather piece. "Here's your sled. Get sliding."

CHAPTER THIRTY

Grant was about to voice his serious objection to sliding down a fecal matter aqueduct on a scrap of dinosaur skin. Then the cries of multiple Coelophyses ripped through the air. Heads bobbed on the far side of the building rubble, searching for prey.

Grant did not want to become prey.

A thousand years of running water had smoothed the stone to a slick surface. Priya climbed onto the aqueduct and seated herself on a leather square. With a couple of pulls with the soles of her feet, she overcame inertia, and began to slide.

"See," Casey said, "easy as pie."

"Couching this experience in dessert references doesn't make me any happier about it."

Grant looked down and saw Priya halfway to the canyon floor. He leaned back against the wall and took a deep breath.

"Priya's doing fine," Casey said.

"Priya weighs a hundred pounds and is nimble. I weigh, well, slightly more than that and can fall off a tricycle."

"Stay here with your dinosaurs, then," Casey said.

He crawled over to the chute and seated himself on the leather. With his heavier weight, it just took one kick to get him sliding down.

The plaza shifted again. Loose rock fell from the top of the wall and bounced off Grant's head. He rubbed his scalp to check for blood and felt something drip on the back of his hand.

He looked up to see a dinosaur looking down at him. Drool dripped from its open mouth. Its gleaming teeth were razor sharp.

Suddenly the idea of sliding down a poop trough sounded fantastic.

He scrambled across the plaza to the chute. The dinosaur's head darted down after him. But the rubble it stood on was unstable. Broken bricks beneath its feet shifted and the creature struggled for balance before toppling over. It rolled down the ruins of the building and off the plaza's edge. A diminishing roar followed it as it plummeted to the canyon floor.

But Grant wasn't any safer. A second dinosaur came running around the rubble's edge and saw Grant immediately. Evaluating whether this was a sign of cooperative hunting would have been interesting had he not been the one being hunted.

He clambered into the chute and sat on the leather square. The smell was oh-so-much worse this close. Priya had tucked into the chute and ridden the dino hide like a bobsled. Casey had pinned his elbows to his side and hunched his shoulders to do about the same. Grant's wide middle touched the side of the cliff. Even if his spare-tire mid-section didn't act like a brake and keep him from sliding, it was going to be one big road rash by the time he got to the bottom.

The dinosaur on the plaza charged, claws scraping against the stone as it lowered its head and aimed it straight for Grant.

Grant leaned out away from the wall. This gave him an awful, direct downward view of the drop off the cliff. His gorge rose, though whether from the stink of the chute or fear of the drop was a toss-up. He threw his weight forward to get moving.

Nothing happened.

Another dinosaur raised its head above the rubble and began a race with the first for a Grant-based lunch. Whichever one won, he would surely lose.

The whole village structure rumbled and shifted. The section of the chute Grant was on heaved upward and sent him sliding forward. Behind him, dinosaurs shrieked. Stone sanded leather and Grant accelerated.

Forward motion was one thing. Control was something else. Grant's shirt tore as he glanced against the cliff face. He leaned further out and an updraft hit him in the face.

As he reeled back from that, he began to rotate sideways. He pressed a heel against the corner of the chute to stay straight. The immediate reward was the smell of the sole of his shoe melting and a shooting pain in his knee.

The leather under his butt began to warm. The edges of the square slipped against his sweaty fingers. He held tighter and pulled in. That flexed his elbows out and one glanced against the cliff face with a cracking noise that promised a terrible reveal at the bottom of this chute, if he was still alive at that point.

He leaned further out over the abyss and tucked his other foot inside the chute. This was as close to holding a sit-up as he'd done since high school and his stomach muscles, such as he had, wailed about trying it now. They rebelled and he inadvertently leaned back.

The chute side grazed his shoulder with all the subtlety of a band saw. That sent Grant back to a sitting position and another bounce off the cliff wall.

He hit a joint in the chute where the next section had dropped.

Grant flew from the chute like a stunt car off a ramp. Airborne, the hot leather square flapped against his butt. He guessed he was about to ride this poor excuse for a flying carpet straight to the canyon bottom.

Instead, he slammed down on the other side of the chute. The impact sent his upper teeth into his lower lip and the coppery taste of his own warm blood made everything even worse.

Grant resigned himself to the fact that there was no way he was going to live through this.

He glanced between his knees. The canyon bottom was coming up fast. Now he realized braking was something he'd need to do, and he had no good way to do it.

He pressed both feet flat against the chute sides. That made the smell of his melting soles stronger, but didn't seem to slow him down. The ground came up fast and his view turned into tunnel vision of the scene of his imminent death. He hoped like hell he could have the heart-attack his body weight owed him before he splattered.

His feet hit a deep crack in the chute. The toes of his shoes caught on the crevice. The rest of him did not. He pivoted up into a standing position and then flew forward, arms outstretched like an ungainly, out-of-shape Superman.

He hit the ground hard. In a classic belly flop, he landed face-first with limbs spread wide on ground that was surprisingly soft. Not that it still didn't hurt like hell. He rolled over and spat some earth from his lips. He was a mass of scrapes and bruises.

"What do you know," he said. "Still not dead."

Casey and Priya ran up on either side of him.

"Grant?" Casey said. "Did you break anything?"

"Just what was left of my spirit."

"You should have started braking a lot sooner," Priya said.

"I'll try and do better next time."

"Another re-discovered native custom just saved your life." Priya's new-found discovery seemed to excite her much more than Grant's survival. "This was their compost heap! We didn't know this concept had been mastered so early."

"A million-to-one shot that it would happen to be here where I needed it," Grant said.

"Oh, no," Priya said. "It makes perfect sense to have it be at the bottom of the waste chute. It saved so much effort."

Grant's jaw sagged. "You mean I'm lying in…"

"Decades of decaying poop," Casey finished for him.

Casey and Priya reached down and helped him up. He was covered in dirt that, unbelievably, smelled worse than the chute he'd slid down on. He checked the others out and they were much cleaner. "How come you're not dirty?"

"We stopped at the bottom of the chute."

"Well, the two of you missed the best part of the experience." Grant brushed some dirt from his shirt. He could see the river from here. "If it wasn't for phytosaurs, I'd sure want to wash some of this off at the river."

"We should probably risk it," Casey said. "That chute ride has the potential of making us all damn sick."

"Species *are* more likely to cluster upstream where water is the cleanest," Grant said. "And the Coelophyses will have them scrambling for cover."

"Plus, we could all use something to drink," Priya said.

"But we'll have to settle for water," Grant said.

From above them came the sound of crumbling rock. Grant looked up the cliff to the village a few hundred yards further north. The remains of the plaza and the buildings on it leaned away from the cliff, and then began what looked like a slow-motion tumble down. With loud crashes and booms, the larger pieces smashed and shattered against the cliff wall. The further the structures fell the more they turned into a dusty, rocky avalanche.

It piled up at the base of the cliff beneath a thick, brown dust cloud.

"A literal housing market crash," Grant said.

Priya sighed. "Answers to so many mysteries are gone forever."

"We were lucky to get out alive," Casey said.

"So did a lot of Coelophyses before the steps down the cliff collapsed," Grant said. "When all those dinosaurs meet, it'll make a shark feeding frenzy look like a diplomat's state dinner."

CHAPTER THIRTY-ONE

An open swath of rocky soil led down to the river from where they stood.

"At least we have a clear path to the river," Grant said.

"It could be that the local tribe cleared this area," Priya said, "maybe used it for planting, or just beaten it clear over time bringing water from the river to the hoist and pulley at the village."

"More likely that the village in the sky changed the runoff pattern during the monsoon season," Casey said. "It collected and concentrated the rainwater, then sent it this way to scour away the prime topsoil here."

Grant smiled at how everyone's specialty colored their theory. The anthropologist blamed people. The geologist blamed the weather. Grant's theory was that frequent visits by phytosaurs had denuded the place.

But for him to be right, the creatures would likely be around now, which meant that there would be Coelophyses arriving here soon to hunt them. He kept his hypothesis to himself and hoped that he was wrong.

The trio soon made it to the riverbank. The first thing Grant checked for was dinosaur footprints in the soft earth. He found none and for once was thrilled to have a theory be incorrect.

The location had an unimpeded view all the way up the canyon. Though the sky here was a cloudless blue, dark thunderheads swelled in the sky north of the canyon. The river ran fast here, but a few boulders that had sheared off the cliff face long ago had rolled into the water on this side and created a calmer, shallow spot. Giant water hyacinths crowded the shoreline.

"If I was one of the native elders," Priya said, "I'd have picked this spot for gathering water for the village."

"As one of the trapped academics," Grant said, "I'm picking this spot for washing off the waste of generations of village elders."

They went to the water's edge and Grant stepped in. The water was cool, but nowhere near as cold as mountain streams he'd visited. He waded through the hyacinths and to the edge of the calmer water. It ended up being about waist deep. He took off his glasses, held them up, and then dunked his head. Everything about the chilly water rinsing filth from his skin felt invigorating. He scrubbed the fingers of his free hand through his hair to loosen up any dirt there. He surfaced and exhaled hard.

He put his glasses back on and saw his two compadres near the shore. They'd gone about knee deep in the water after taking off their shoes. They were giving him and the whole river very wary looks.

"Fear of disease trumps fear of phytosaurs, huh?" Casey said.

"Pass me a bar of soap and I'll make a day of it in here."

Grant ducked down neck deep and tried to get the current to do most of the scrubbing work. When he thought he was as rinsed as he was going to get, he stood up and sloshed ashore to where the other two sat on a boulder with wet faces and hands. Water streamed from over his stomach and splattered on his shoes.

"Having washed the literal dirt of ages from me," Grant said, "I feel better."

"You want to lay those clothes out to dry?" Casey said as he pointed to a boulder in the sun.

The idea of having his pale, rotund body even partially exposed in front of Priya made him ill.

"I'll stick with soggy," Grant said. "I'm starting to like it."

"You have a strange sense of humor," Priya said.

Since he had rarely seen her smile, Grant wondered what her frame of reference was for a *good* sense of humor.

"So now what do we do?" Grant said. "The village in the sky is destroyed. The worksite is a dinosaur hunting ground. These cliffs are as sheer as the ones further north."

"Our only hope is to wait for Neoborax to show up and hope they find us," Casey said.

Grant pulled two crushed and soggy protein bars from his pocket. "Dinner's on me while we wait."

"Thanks for the reminder that we'll starve to death before we're rescued," Priya said.

"Some slower than others," Casey said, smiling at Grant.

"You're jealous because my decision to delay starting my diet worked in my favor."

Priya sighed. "If all these creatures never got out of here, neither will we."

"At least we found someplace safe for now," Grant said.

A phytosaur shrieked just upstream. Everyone jumped to their feet.

"Are you some mystical jinx?" Casey said.

The trees just upstream of them shook. Then a phytosaur crashed through them and rolled sideways across the riverbank. It stopped on its feet just yards away. Gashes in its back oozed bright, red blood. The creature spun around to face upriver. Its tail whipped past the trio and sent a spray of dirt in their faces.

The clash of the dinosaurs had found them.

CHAPTER THIRTY-TWO

The three of them ducked behind a boulder near the river.

Then a Coelophysis sprinted out of the woods. Blood covered its flanks and it was bigger than any of the ones Grant had seen so far. It leapt and landed on the back of the phytosaur. Its great claws dug in deep and it clamped its jaws around the phytosaur's broad neck. Teeth dug in and the phytosaur screamed.

What would have been a killing bite to any animal on the planet was far from that against the thick, armored neck of the phytosaur. It thrashed back and forth to dislodge the attacker. But the Coelophysis hung on. This was no fight between a predator and prey. This was two top predators in a struggle to the death.

The phytosaur changed tactics. Using its tail for leverage, it rolled toward the river. Grant had seen modern crocodiles use this same move, but underwater to subdue prey. On the ground it might save the creature's life. At the first revolution, Grant was sure that the weight of the phytosaur would crush the slimmer, lighter Coelophysis. But as the phytosaur rolled back up on its feet, the assailant had hung on with the tenacity of a bull rider. It roared through clenched jaws and shook its head, trying to work its teeth deeper into its victim's skin.

The phytosaur barely paused. It tried the roll again and splashed into the river. Both creatures sank below the rushing water.

Fifty feet downstream, they surfaced as a thrashing mass of white water and reptile skin. It was hard to tell one creature from the other as the current swept them away. At the end of the canyon, the river sucked them into the hole that took the flow back underground.

Before Grant could comment about how lucky they'd been, that luck evaporated.

Several phytosaurs came charging from the woods, sending trees and branches crashing to the ground. They zigzagged across the open space. Then two Coelophyses came sprinting after them. The area on the other side of the rock turned into a roaring, shrieking melee. Dinosaurs leapt and rolled as the creatures fought for survival.

Coelophyses jumped atop phytosaurs or chomped on their legs. The slower phytosaurs used their powerful tails to batter the assailants and knock them free of other victims. Reptile roars punctuated the air and gouts of blood splattered the earth.

Grant and the others bolted from the fighting dinosaurs. They ran south along the riverbank. The forest grew denser and as soon as the cries of the wounded dinosaurs sounded distant enough, Grant called a wheezing halt to the retreat. He bent over and rested his hands on his knees. The others came to his side.

"You guys..." Grant sucked in a deep breath, "... looked like you needed a break."

"It's chaos up there," Casey said.

"Predators have scattered the phytosaurs across the valley," Grant said. "They'll hunt them until there aren't any left to eat."

"Then maybe they'll hunt each other," Priya said.

"Only after they've hunted us," Grant said.

"There's nowhere to hide," Priya said, "and no way out of here."

"I have a very bad idea," Casey said. "There's one way out. We leave the way the river does."

"Through the hole in the canyon wall?" Priya said. "We don't even know where the water goes."

"It sure as hell goes somewhere other than here," Casey said.

"But it does it underground," Grant said.

"That doesn't mean it isn't traveling through survivable caverns," Casey said. "There are plenty of underground rivers in this area that have carved out large channels in the sandstone over time. The recent drought here means it's even more likely we'll be able to swim with open space and breathable air above."

"I hate to agree with a geologist on anything," Grant said, "but you may be right. One problem. Despite the promise of my lithe figure, I'm not a strong swimmer."

"Even a strong swimmer would get sucked under in that river," Priya said. "We saw the fighting dinosaurs get pulled under."

Casey snapped his fingers. "The giant water hyacinths! We'll rip free some of the floating bladders and use them to stay above the water."

"Like life rings," Priya said, "but without the hole."

Grant wanted to add "and without a weight rating." Sure, one of those could keep little Priya afloat, but keeping his cheeseburger-produced butt above water was another thing entirely.

"It's going to take some convincing to get me bouncing down a set of rapids into a dark hole in the ground," Grant said.

A dinosaur roar split the air nearby. Grant whirled to see a Coelophysis bound out to the riverbank. It had a bloody phytosaur leg in its mouth. This fight was spilling south faster than he'd expected.

"Okay," Grant said. "Now I'm convinced."

The three ran for the water hyacinth patch along the riverbank. Here the bladders were about three feet long and two feet wide, attached to a labyrinth of hyacinth leaves with a single coarse stem. Grant waded in to the nearest one. He pressed it down into the water and it popped back up. The casing seemed pretty tough.

He looked across to Priya. She lay atop one bladder with it tucked between her chin and her chest. She floated easily.

Grant lay on the bladder near him and went under in an instant. He stood back up spitting water from his mouth.

"Okay," he said to himself, "so I need two."

He followed the stem down to where it joined the plant underwater. A sharp tug tore it free.

A second Coelophysis made it to the riverbank. The first creature roared at the newcomer, as if declaring its intention to keep its phytosaur leg to itself. The second dinosaur backed away, then caught sight of the three people in the river.

"Company's coming," Grant said.

The dinosaur sprinted for the trio. Holding the first bladder stem in one hand, Grant hunted for the stem to another bladder. He found one, grabbed it, and pulled.

But messing with the first one had made his hand slimy. The stem slipped through his fingers. He wrapped the stem around his hand and yanked even harder. The stem felt like it was going to garrot off his fingers. But the damn thing didn't break.

Casey and Priya had already launched into the river. That left Grant the only available dinosaur dinner, and the creature was heading right for him.

Grant straddled the stem with his back to the leaves. He took a deep breath and pulled. The leaves moved closer and gave him the wedgie of a lifetime. But then the stem broke.

He wound the stems around his hands until he'd reeled in the two floating bladders. He tucked one under each arm, prayed they were buoyant enough, and pushed out into the river.

He sank.

But then he pulled the bladders closer, to under his chest, and his head broke above the water. From shore behind him came the roar of the frustrated Coelophysis. Grant kicked with all his might.

And barely moved. He really was as poor a swimmer as he'd remembered.

He kept kicking and added a ridiculous-looking inchworm-like undulation to his body in the hope that would help.

The attacking dinosaur splashed into the river, trampling water lilies. It would be on Grant in a second and his kicking wasn't going to save him.

But the river did. He hit the edge of the fast current. It ran under the bladders, lifted them, and then pushed them downstream. Grant clung on for his life as the frustrated dinosaur he'd left behind shrieked its displeasure.

Relief at his escape released so much tension, he almost let the bladders go. Grant glanced over his shoulder at the dinosaur waist-deep in the river.

"Mammals rule, loser."

The river whisked him away and the dinosaur spun around and bounded off in search of other prey. Grant turned to face downstream and his heart jumped into his throat.

He was a foot away from the hole in the canyon wall.

CHAPTER THIRTY-THREE

Casey had been right about one thing. The river had hollowed itself out a nice underground tunnel. As Grant slipped through the opening, there was a foot or two of headroom between the water and the tunnel ceiling. For now.

The speed of the water increased as the river narrowed into the underwater channel. The surface got choppier and splashed Grant in the face as he tried to stay upright in the increasingly turbulent flow. The rush of water against the sandstone sides made a whooshing noise that created a disorienting echo.

What Casey hadn't mentioned was that once the river left the opening, the tunnel was engulfed in the most absolute level of darkness Grant had ever experienced.

After the last bit of light from the entrance winked out, Grant lost track of all orientation. Up, down, forward, backward. Motion had no meaning as he bobbed and bounced along in the river. Occasional glancing blows reminded him that he could crash into a very solid wall if this river took a sharp turn up ahead.

An even worse realization took hold. The channel could narrow without warning, the life-sustaining air space above him disappear, and the river end up spitting his lifeless corpse out wherever it exited. He closed his eyes and held the bladders tightly.

With a muffled boom, one bladder popped.

The current sucked Grant under like a vacuum cleaner. The sound of rushing water surrounded him now and seemed to echo in his head. Water pressure pressed against his chest and conspired with his oxygen-starved lungs to demand fresh air. He felt certain he was tumbling in the current. He knew that any moment now he'd break a limb crashing into stone, smash his head against an outcrop, or surrender to his lungs' screaming order to exhale.

His back slammed hard into a wall. Grant's mouth opened and a torrent of bubbles rushed by his face. Water blasted down his throat and he gagged.

Reality began to seem fuzzy. He hoped his life wasn't about to flash before his eyes, because he'd hate to have to watch that sad movie as his last living act.

Before that show could start, he lost consciousness.

***

It was just as people had described it. Darkness with a light shining overhead in the distance. Grant was having the near-death experience so many had written about. In moments, he'd know the answers to so many unanswered questions.

A hand slapped his face hard. "Wake up, damn it!"

Grant's eyes focused. Priya knelt beside him. He rolled over and threw up more water than he thought a human body could hold. He returned to his back and went limp.

"Now I know what a washcloth feels like after all the water gets wrung out of it," Grant said. "We aren't both dead, are we? Because if this is what dead feels like, eternity is going to be miserable."

"No," Priya said. "All three of us are still alive."

Grant sat up. Before he could stop it, he threw up some more water all over his shirt. A symphony of spastic hacking added even more embarrassment to his situation. When he stopped, he looked around to see where he was.

They were in a cave. The air was humid and heavy, tinged with the scent of a multitude of minerals. At his feet, the river still rushed by. Casey was there, standing a few feet from Grant, wiping water from his pants and shirt. The three sat on a wide rock slab that angled down toward the river. The higher end butted up against a pile of other boulders that rose to the cavern ceiling. At the top of that pile was the reason he could see anything. Light blazed in from a hole in the cavern ceiling. Deep shadows on the other side hinted that the cave stretched even further back.

"Where are we?" Grant said.

"A cave the river carved out long ago." Casey walked up the slab to where it met the pile of boulders. "These rocks in the pile are sharp and clean, the remnants of two ceiling collapses. Probably the work of the recent detonation of charges Neoborax was doing."

"You fished me out of the river?" Grant said to Priya.

"She fished us both out," Casey said.

"Way to keep my ex-wife's alimony payments coming, Priya," Grant said. "Seriously, thank you."

Priya pointed to the hole way up in the ceiling. "And it looks like we may have a way out of here,"

"Not *we*," Casey said.

He pulled a black pistol from the big pocket on the side of his cargo pants. He pointed it at the two of them as he backed away to the edge of the slab.

"Casey," Grant said. "What are you doing?"

"I'm getting rich. This disaster is still going to be my ticket to an early retirement."

"I don't understand," Priya said. "You think Neoborax is going to pay you more now?"

"Not Neoborax. One of its competitors. The day after Neoborax approached me about this expedition, so did a representative of another firm. If this was a place worth mining, and I could help them claim it before Neoborax did, my cut of the monthly gross would be staggering."

"Normally, I'd be happy that you double-crossed those double-crossers," Grant said. "But since you're pointing a gun at me, my support is a little dampened."

"Casey, you must have cheered every time bad luck set back the Neoborax group," Priya said.

"Luck? I wasn't going to count on that. Who do you think set off the explosion in the canyon rim camp?"

Grant remembered how Casey had hung back before the trip to the canyon floor, and how he'd been the last to come down. "You blew up their little ammo dump?"

"All my coal mining experience finally served a purpose. You'd be shocked at how easy it is to pick up some explosives expertise. That came in handy again when I booby trapped the charges that Terri brought up to the village in the sky."

"So she didn't blow herself up by accident?"

"Technically, she did blow herself up, but not by accident. I figured that she'd open her pack somewhere, but I never bargained for her doing it in the nest room. But I lived through it. She had to go, though. With her dead, my company could get their claim in while Neoborax still wondered about the fate of their people." Casey pulled a wad of soggy papers from another pocket and threw them on the ground. "And no one's ever going to find the notes Kraus left at the worksite, even if they do get down there. It will all be a big, mysterious tragedy."

Grant had another dark revelation. "And Kraus didn't fall off the observation point, did he?"

"Again, technically, he fell. After being pushed. All of you caught me on the way back to my room, but I played the concerned citizen well enough that you thought I was checking on who screamed."

"But before we arrived, you couldn't have known there were dinosaurs in the canyon," Priya said.

"No, that was a real surprise. But I figured that would work in my favor if they wrecked Neoborax's operation."

Grant felt like he'd been sucker-punched. Something else occurred to him. "Don't tell me you dug up all the missing charges from around the worksite."

"After I disarmed them, I found a nice, safe spot to wait for the phytosaurs to rush in and kill you all." Casey laughed. "You all actually thought the dinosaurs dug them up. Animals with brains the size of an apple understood how to disarm and dispose of plastic explosives? How dumb can you be?"

"I can't believe you're doing this," Grant said.

"Oh, you can't believe that struggling on a professor's salary for decades has driven me to accept a shortcut to cash when one is offered? Hey, I don't have book deals hosing money into my bank account like you do."

"I think 'dripping' is a more accurate description," Grant said. "And while we were being threatened by Terri and Kraus, you had a gun this whole time?"

"My ace in the hole for the final hand." Casey smiled and patted his other pocket. "And I have a satellite phone. With which I'll call for a ride once I'm back topside."

"Why did you drag the two of us into this mess with you?" Priya said.

"Later, when my double-cross came to light," Casey said, "I'd have plausible deniability. Much more likely one of you two sold out Neoborax."

"We don't care who you tell about the canyon uranium," Priya said. "Whatever story you spin is fine with us. We just want to get back to our normal lives."

"Sadly," Grant said, "this whole trip has been way too much like my normal life."

"I can't take that risk," Casey said. "Grant here will probably turn the whole thing into one of his stupid novels."

"And I'll change everyone's name but yours," Grant said.

"Rest assured," Casey said as he backed up to the bottom of the boulder pile, "in the story I tell, you'll both be heroic. Just not as heroic as the sole survivor."

A deep hiss came from the dark depths at the far end of the cave. Grant's heart skipped a beat as he recognized the sound. Casey spun around.

A phytosaur materialized out of the black recess. Deep, awful wounds gouged its neck and back. Grant recognized it as the phytosaur that had been swept into the river with the attacking Coelophysis.

Casey fired one useless round at the creature, then started a mad scramble up the mountain of fallen rock.

The phytosaur charged after him. It raced up the slab and onto the rock pile. Its clawed feet sent loose rocks tumbling in all directions as it pursued Casey.

With the gun in one hand, Casey could barely climb. The phytosaur closed rapidly. Casey made the mistake of turning to look back. He saw the creature closing in and screamed.

That was all the delay the dinosaur needed.

It caught up, spread its jaws, and clamped them around Casey's midsection. The professor wailed and blood pumped from both sides of the dinosaur's mouth.

But the dinosaur couldn't savor its meal. The unstable rocks beneath its feet broke free. The phytosaur windmilled its legs which only sent more rocks tumbling. The dinosaur lost its grip and slid down the rock pile sideways, straight for the river.

It was also heading straight for Grant and Priya.

Grant jumped up and grabbed Priya around the waist. He held her close, dropped on one shoulder and skidded across the flat stone with the help of his slimy, soaked clothes. He stopped when his back hit the side of the cave.

The dinosaur slid past them. The closest foot passed inches from Grant's face and its claws left deep gouges in the sandstone surface. It spun into the water with its head facing upstream and Casey's body still between its jaws. The water pushed the creature under, and the current swept it down into the river's dark passage.

Grant felt Priya's heart hammer against his chest. He let Priya go. She rolled across the rock and sat up.

"That was close," she said. "You saved my life."

"Well, you fished me out of that river, so I thought I owed you one."

"I thought you and Casey were good friends."

"So did I. You just never know who someone really is until you're trapped in a canyon full of dinosaurs together, I guess."

The two rose to their feet. Grant couldn't pinpoint any part of his body that didn't hurt.

"How about we climb up and out of here?" Priya said.

"I'd prefer to use the escalator, but I can't seem to find it. After you, then."

CHAPTER THIRTY-FOUR

Grant had rationalized that letting Priya climb out first was the gentlemanly thing to do. In the event she slipped, he would be there to catch her and save her from a grievous injury.

In reality, he'd made the choice so he could save his ego from a grievous injury. He didn't want her watching every grunt, groan, and wheeze as he tried to scale the rubble mountain.

As luck would have it, Grant didn't fall far behind. Priya took care in choosing the best route up, pausing often. That gave Grant time to catch-up even though he was doing what was close to a caterpillar crawl.

As they climbed, the air became hotter and drier. The stale smell of the desert began to replace the stagnant scent of the river cavern. Once at the top, in what Grant believed was his only lucky break during this entire misadventure, the opening to the surface was only a foot above the topmost boulder. They were going to get out of here after all.

Priya made it to the opening first. She stuck the upper half of her body through, and then returned with a huge smile. "Open desert. No canyon. No dinosaurs."

"At this point," Grant said, "that's one burger joint away from being heaven."

Priya crawled through to the other side. Grant went to follow her, and stopped just short of the opening as he noticed a problem. He wasn't going to fit.

Priya stuck her head back through. "Decided you prefer the cave?"

"That opening looks tight. I take a 40-inch waist."

She gave him a look of disbelief.

"Well, I did at one point. Suffice it to say, it's larger than that opening."

"Then we need to make it bigger."

Priya crawled back into the cave. She picked up a sparkling black and white rock with a pointed end that was about the size of a grapefruit. "Find some quartz like this and get to work."

Priya sat beside one side of the opening and began to smash the rock against the sandstone rim. The harder quartz broke bits of the softer stone away with each blow.

Grant rooted around in the pile until he found a similarly colored chunk of rock. He went to work on the other side of the opening.

"That nest cave we found," Priya said. "This is how the first tribe carved it out."

"I've just become a big fan of jackhammers."

"I have one of my classes do a lab like this, where they have to create and use stone tools. By seeing what designs work best, they can better recognize neolithic tools when they find them."

"That's a class I won't be auditing."

"I'll give you life experience credit for it."

They beat away at the rock a little while longer. Grant began to sweat and even though he switched hands regularly, both of them soon ached under the strain.

"You should base your next book on what we've been through," Priya said.

"You knew about my books before we came down here?"

"I've read some of them," she said. "I have to confess that mindless genre fiction is my guilty pleasure."

"I'll pretend that's a compliment."

"It will be different basing the story on a real experience for once."

"Yeah," Grant said, "real different."

"What *are* we going to say happened here?" Priya said.

"A lot less than what actually happened."

Priya struck the opening on her side. With a loud crack, a substantial piece of sandstone fell away. She and Grant pitched in and rolled it out of the opening. It bounced down the rock pile, into the darkness, and eventually made a splash as it ended up in the river. The opening was now a Grant-sized hole.

"Let's go," Grant said.

Priya went through first. Grant followed her. He did still have to suck in his gut, but he tried not to be obvious about it. On the other side, Priya helped him to his feet. The cave opening was in the side of a small hill. He stood and winked against the sunlight.

Indeed, they stood in a stretch of Utah desert. Far west of them, purple mountains sat beneath a clear blue sky. There wasn't a sign of life anywhere.

"This is desolate," Grant said. "But at least nothing's trying to eat us."

"You two look awful," a little girl's voice said behind them.

Grant turned to see a little girl in shorts and a t-shirt wearing oversized sunglasses and a floppy hat. She stood atop the little hill they'd just crawled out of.

Grant and Priya looked each other over. The girl was right. Their clothes were torn, they were soaking wet, and scrapes and bruises covered their bodies.

"Where are your parents?" Grant asked.

The girl hooked a thumb over her shoulder. "Over here."

They climbed the rise and followed the girl a hundred feet to where a Jeep was parked between two blue tents. A young man and woman sat in folding chairs by the Jeep. The two of them could have passed for Haight Ashbury hippies in 1968. At the sight of Grant and Priya they both stood up.

"Look, Daddy," the girl said. "They're mole people."

"Come here, Kara," the woman called. Kara ran to her mother's side.

The man looked the two of them up and down with a wary eye. "Where did you come from?"

"A hole in the ground at the base of this hill," Grant said.

"So you *are* mole people?"

"No, college professors who got turned around exploring some caves. What would it take to get a ride back to the closest bit of civilization?"

CHAPTER THIRTY-FIVE

Their ride back to civilization didn't get all the way there. The road their hippie savior selected drove near the Neoborax worksite. Several vehicles were parked there, including one from the State Police. Grant and Priya decided that the presence of the police would guarantee their safety, so they had their driver let them out and they walked back to the base camp.

They kept their story simple. Two days ago, they had just arrived at the camp. The two of them were at the canyon rim admiring the view a hundred yards north of the camp. There was an explosion. They ran back, found no one alive, saw that all the ropes to the people down below were gone. They had no way to call for help, so decided to try and walk back to the main road and flag down a car. They got turned around, never found the road, and finally made it back to the camp.

Grant and Priya stuck to this story when being questioned by the police, who were much more interested in having Neoborax explain the undocumented explosives on site. They still stuck to it later, under more intensive questioning by Neoborax men. It was clear they were concerned that the two had discovered some of the secrets of the site, but Grant and Priya played dumb and the men bought it.

Grant did manage to slip in how disappointed Kraus and Terri were about what a waste of time the trip had been for them and how unstable the canyon walls were. No point in having the Neoborax people decide Desolation Canyon was worth another expedition.

***

Two weeks later at Robeson College, there was a campus-wide period of mourning for poor Casey, tragically lost on the expedition. Grant just gritted his teeth through the memorial service at the football stadium. He returned to his office straight away when it finished.

Grant sat behind his desk and whipped off the constricting tie around his neck. He was about to let loose a slew of frustrated profanities when Priya arrived at his door. She still had on the sharp black dress she wore for the service, but also had a satchel in her hand.

This was the first time the two of them had been alone since they met the hippies in the desert. She'd been at the memorial, but on the other side of the stands.

"That was hard to stomach," she said.

"One more compliment for Casey and I would have thrown up," Grant said.

"I knew you were upset. You skipped the hors d'oeuvres set up in the conference room afterwards."

Grant wished she had smiled when she said that.

"The canyon disaster was a loss in many ways," Priya said.

"Yes. It would have been a perfect environment to study two living dinosaur species. But I'm certain that the Coelophyses have wiped out the phytosaurs, then killed each other or died without the life-giving force of the uranium deposits."

"And the village in the sky and any trace of the entire civilization there have been destroyed. I could have spent the rest of my life studying it." Now a smile crossed her face. "But look what I did instead."

She reached into her satchel and pulled out a thick sheaf of typed pages. She dropped it on Grant's desk with a thud. The cover page read:

DANGER IN THE CANYON

By Priya Maharaj

"Don't tell me," Grant said.

"Yes, I wrote a novel based on our experience. I was shocked at how quickly the words came. I wrote almost ten thousand words a day."

Grant's good writing days topped out at under a quarter of that.

"And this week I was able to get an agent, listen in on the bidding war for the publishing rights, and sign a movie option. You never told me getting published was so easy."

Grant grimaced. He'd been writing for years and none of that had ever happened to him. "The stars were certainly aligned for you."

"I have to run. I must get started writing the screenplay. You wouldn't believe how much you get paid to do that."

Grant knew exactly how much one got paid to do that, not that his agent ever managed to get him a contract to do so.

Priya grabbed her manuscript and blew out of the office. Grant slumped in his chair. He pulled open the right top desk drawer and extracted a sloppy pile of fifty typed pages. The title on the first page read:

DESOLATION CANYON

He dropped the whole lot into his wastepaper basket.

***

Later, Grant was ready to lock up his office and call it a miserable day when his phone rang. It was his agent, Harvey. Talking with him promised to be the rancid icing atop the burned cake that had been his day. He answered the phone anyway.

"How's my favorite author?" Harvey said.

"Let me put you on hold," Grant said, "and I'll call Stephen King and find out."

"Now, Grant, you know I mean you. We have that special bond."

"Sealed with a percent of my royalty checks."

"You have a new manuscript coming my way?"

Grant looked at the sheaf of papers in the wastebasket. "It's on its way somewhere."

"The publisher is hitting me up for something new from you. Could be a larger advance if we get him something soon."

Grant sighed and took the manuscript out of the trash.

All I have to do is change the location and the characters and the plot, he thought.

"Speaking of money," Harvey continued, "since you brought it up. Despite you turning down the amazing consulting offer which I debased myself to get you, I have another opportunity, a big one."

"Lay it on me."

"The Adventure Writer's Conference. A convocation of writers who specialize in the adventure story genre. And the featured author is...wait for it... Grant Coleman."

Grant didn't think any group of writers would have standards so low. "Are you serious?"

"As a heart attack. They want writers to teach seminars on the craft. And you're like a teacher in your real-life job, right?"

Grant was thrilled to learn that his agent didn't consider writing Grant's actual job. He looked at the stack of graded tests on his desk. "Yes, my real-life job is something like that."

"And the best part, it's at a high-roller safari resort in Africa, the perfect setting to inspire adventure. Africa's also a whole new market. You don't sell any books in Africa. Millions of potential readers. Make a splash there and we can move the whole back catalog again."

The idea was tempting. His alimony payments were starting to fall behind.

"Where is this place?"

"Langanika."

"Where the hell is Langanika?"

"It's the capital city of the Republic of Simpupu."

"Where the hell is Simpupu?"

"You know what a map of Africa looks like? Well, it's a little country in the middle."

"A safe little country, right?"

"Grant, my dear friend, I'm shocked you would even ask that. The conference is reimbursing all expenses and paying more for a week of non-work than you make in a month."

Grant did like the sound of that offer. He could end up with a little financial breathing room now and some major sales upside later. "Send me everything you have on this offer."

Keyboard keys tapped on the other end of the conversation. "Done. Once more, the world's greatest agent comes through for you. I'll personally make all the reservations, get you the best flights and the finest room. Gotta run. Stay in touch."

Harvey hung up. Grant's phone dinged announcing he had a new email message. He decided to check it when he got home. He'd also do a little research on Simpupu and make sure there hadn't been any sightings of giant monsters. For once he wanted to teach about writing adventure stories, not be inspired to write the next one.

AFTERWORD

Grant managed to get through his seventh adventure and he's "still not dead." I say he is one lucky man. He says unlucky, but he's such a glass half-empty guy.

The inspiration for this novel came during a trip out west to the Mad Monster Party convention in Phoenix, Arizona. I stopped at the New Mexico Museum of Natural History & Science in Albuquerque, New Mexico. What a great museum! They had amazing dinosaur exhibits of creatures that once lived in the Southwest. Two that were featured were the phytosaur and Coelophysis. I wanted to have Grant venture into a desert this time around and one of these two would be a great adversary. I could not decide which, so much to Grant's chagrin, I used both.

Phytosaurs lived in the late Triassic period, about 220 million years ago. Technically they were archosaurs, not dinosaurs. They resembled crocodiles, though crocodiles did not evolve from them. They grew to over ten feet long and munched on fish with the rows of sharp teeth in their long snouts. Their backs were heavily armored, taken as proof that something else out there wanted to eat them. They were widespread across North America.

All the traits I ascribed to phytosaurs were borrowed from crocodile and alligator behavior. They can move very fast when they are on the hunt and they can climb vertical surfaces with the help of their tails. Writing research was my excuse for several visits to Gatorland in Orlando, Florida where all this behavior was observed. Go visit yourself and tell them I sent you. They'll respond by asking "Who the hell is Russell James?"

While phytosaurs have a version that still roams the Earth, be very glad that Coelophysis does not. These dinosaurs were contemporaries of the phytosaurs. Coelophysis is known from a massive death assemblage of hundreds of skeletons found at Ghost Ranch in New Mexico in 1947. They grew to nine feet long and were quick, deadly predators. If you are thinking of the raptors in *Jurassic Park*, you are on the right track. They likely laid eggs like in the novel, and a lot of scientific evidence points to cannibalism when things got tight. The ones in the story are more robust than real-life versions since they had to go after the phytosaurs. I made up the massive growth spurt after hatching.

The idea of a verdant canyon in the desert is not as far-fetched as one might think. While hiking in desolated Arches Canyonland National Park, I came across similar examples. I'd cross a sandy, sunbaked ridge, and in the valley below stood a forest. Large trees, bushes, and grasses clustered around the length of a stream, making a serpentine oasis in the desert. It even created its own cooler micro-climate. Isolated in a canyon, it's conceivable that it could manifest its own ecosystem.

The Neoborax baddies are in search of uranium, and the Southwest was once a great place to find it. After World War II, a lot of uranium mining happened out there. The Four Corners area where Utah, Colorado, Arizona, and New Mexico meet, teemed with prospectors. Between 1946 and 1959, 309,380 claims were filed in four Utah counties alone. As mentioned, there is an abandoned uranium mine in one of the walls of the Grand Canyon. As the easy to reach surface deposits were played out, mining decreased. But there are likely still large deposits underground ready to be discovered.

The "village in the sky" was inspired by the Anasazi people Priya talks about. This tribe in the New Mexico area lived as others did in pre-colonial times. But about 1200 AD, they began to build cliffside dwellings like Grant found in the novel, some of them very complex. Mesa Verde in New Mexico has amazing examples. It is unclear why they thought they needed this highly defensible position, but given the effort to create it, the need had to be great and immediate. Then even stranger, within less than a hundred years, the villages were all abandoned. Evidence of cannibalism has been found at multiple sites.

Theories to explain this strange behavior include environmental collapse, invasion, civil war, and even the rise of a messianic, apocalyptic leader. It may have been a combination of the above. What I'm sure of is it had nothing to do with dinosaurs.

Heartfelt thanks go out to my beta readers Deb deAlteriis and Donna Fitzpatrick who gave Grant's latest story a once over before it went to the presses. And thanks to all the folks at Severed Press who turn my manuscripts into the sharp ebooks, audio books, and paperbacks that you enjoy.

While you await Grant's next adventure, you can entertain yourself with the adventures of Rangers Kathy West and Nathan Toland who fight to keep dangerous creatures at bay in the United States National Park system. In *Claws* they battle giant crabs at Fort Jefferson in the Florida Keys. In *Dragons of Kilauea*, fire-breathing giant Komodo dragons threaten Volcanoes National Park in Hawaii. In their latest adventure, *Ravens of Yellowstone*, they discover the secrets of the park system's formation while uncovering a roost of murderous birds about to be set free.

You can also try Rick and Rose Sinclair's adventures. In 1938, these antique store owners end up on quests to find lost treasures and artifacts. In *Quest for the Queen's Temple* they search for the lost treasury of the Queen of Sheba. In *Voyage to Blackbeard's Island* it's a search for pirate treasure. Both series are available from Severed Press at booksellers around the world.

Stay well and keep reading. Feel free to visit my website at http://www.russellrjames.com, follow on Twitter @RRJames14, or say hello at Russell R. James or Russell James- Author on Facebook. You can also sign up for a free monthly newsletter at this link.

https://landing.mailerlite.com/webforms/landing/i5k2m1.

See you for Grant's next adventure.

-Russell James

Checkout other great books by bestselling author

Greig Beck

PRIMORDIA: IN SEARCH OF THE LOST WORLD

Ben Cartwright, former soldier, home to mourn the loss of his father stumbles upon cryptic letters from the past between the author, Arthur Conan Doyle and his great, great grandfather who vanished while exploring the Amazon jungle in 1908. Amazingly, these letters lead Ben to believe that his ancestor's expedition was the basis for Doyle's fantastical tale of a lost world inhabited by long extinct creatures. As Ben digs some more he finds clues to the whereabouts of a lost notebook that might contain a map to a place that is home to creatures that would rewrite everything known about history, biology and evolution. But other parties now know about the notebook, and will do anything to obtain it. For Ben and his friends, it becomes a race against time and against ruthless rivals. In the remotest corners of Venezuela, along winding river trails known only to lost tribes, and through near impenetrable jungle, Ben and his novice team find a forbidden place more terrifying and dangerous than anything they could ever have imagined.

THE FOSSIL

Klaus and Doris have just made the discovery of their lives – a complete Neanderthal skeleton buried in a newly opened sinkhole. But on removing it, something else tumbles free. Something that switches on, and then calls home.Soon the owners are coming back, and nothing will stop their ruthless search for their lost prize. Gruesome corpses begin to pile up, and Detective Ed Heisner of the Berlin Police is assigned to a case like nothing he has ever experienced before in his life. Heisner must stay one step ahead of a group of secretive Special Forces soldiers also tracking the strange device, while trying to find an unearthly group of killers that are torturing, burning, and obliterating their victims all the way across the city.THE FOSSIL is a time jumping detective novella where humans soon find that time can be the greatest weapon of all.* THE FOSSIL first appeared in SNAFU No.1 (2014) as a short story. Due to numerous requests, it has now been expanded and released here in its complete, stand-alone novella form.

Check out other great

Dinosaur Thrillers!

Rick Poldark

PRIMORDIAL ISLAND

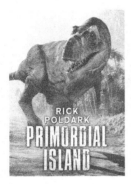

During a violent storm Flight 207 crash-lands in the South China Sea. Poseidon Tech tracks the wreckage to an uncharted island and dispatches a curious salvage team—two paleontologists, a biologist specializing in animal behavior, a botanist, and a nefarious big game hunter. Escorted by a heavily-armed security team, they cut through the jungle and quickly find themselves in a terrifying fight for survival, running a deadly gauntlet of prehistoric predators. In their quest for the flight recorder, they uncover the mystery of the island's existence and discover an arcane force that will tip the balance of power on the primordial island. Things are not as they seem as they race against time to survive the island's man-eating dinosaurs and make it back home in one piece.

P.K. Hawkins

SUBTERRANEA

Fall, 1985. The small town of Kettle Hollow barely shows up on any maps, and four young friends are used to taking their BMX's outside of town in an effort to find anything interesting to do. But tonight their tendency to go off by themselves may have saved them, and also forced them into the adventure of a lifetime.While they were away, Kettle Hollow has been locked down by the government, and a portal to another world has opened on Main Street. It's a world deep below the ground, a world where dinosaurs roam free, where giant plants and mutant insects hunt for prey. It's also a world where all their family and friends have been kidnapped for sinister purposes. Now, with time running out before the portal closes, the four friends must brave the unknown to save their loved ones. Time is running out, and in the darkened tunnels of Subterranea, something is hunting them.

 SEVERED**PRESS**

CHECK OUT OTHER GREAT DINOSAUR BOOKS

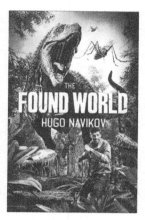

THE FOUND WORLD
by **Hugo Navikov**

A powerful global cabal wants adventurer Brett Russell to retrieve a superweapon stolen by the scientist who built it. To entice him to travel underneath one of the most dangerous volcanoes on Earth to find the scientist, this shadowy organization will pay him the only thing he cares about: information that will allow him to avenge his family's murder.

But before he can get paid, he and his team must enter an underground hellscape of killer plants, giant insects, terrifying dinosaurs, and an army of other predators never previously seen by man.

At the end of this journey awaits a revelation that could alter the fate of mankind ... if they can make it back from this horrifying found world.

HOUSE OF THE GODS
by **Davide Mana**

High above the steamy jungle of the Amazon basin, rise the flat plateaus known as the Tepui, the House of the Gods. Lost worlds of unknown beauty, a naturalistic wonder, each an ecology onto itself, shunned by the local tribes for centuries. The House of the Gods was not made for men.

But now, the crew and passengers of a small charter plane are about to find what was hidden for sixty million years.

Lost on an island in the clouds 10.000 feet above the jungle, surrounded by dinosaurs, hunted by mysterious mercenaries, the survivors of Sligo Air flight 001 will quickly learn the only rule of life on Earth: Extinction.

Made in the USA
Monee, IL
16 September 2024

65889431R00095